Gurdon S. Hubbard, Henry E. Hamilton

Incidents and Events in the Life of Gurdon Saltonstall Hubbard

Volume 1

Gurdon S. Hubbard, Henry E. Hamilton

Incidents and Events in the Life of Gurdon Saltonstall Hubbard
Volume 1

ISBN/EAN: 9783337329679

Printed in Europe, USA, Canada, Australia, Japan

Cover: Foto ©Andreas Hilbeck / pixelio.de

More available books at **www.hansebooks.com**

INCIDENTS AND EVENTS

IN THE LIFE OF

GURDON SALTONSTALL HUBBARD.

COLLECTED FROM PERSONAL NARRATIONS AND OTHER SOURCES.

AND ARRANGED BY HIS NEPHEW,

HENRY E. HAMILTON.

1888.

Printers, Engravers and Electrotypers
Chicago.

CONTENTS.

The following pages are partly autobiographical, and partly compiled from the narrations of Mr. Hubbard, and from letters and other documents written during the years of which they treat. They make no claim to literary merit; neither do romance nor imagination have any place in the story. It is the simple recital of some events in the early life of Mr. Hubbard, which show the many perils through which he passed and the various hardships which he endured.

That these events occurred where great centres of civilization now exist, and during the lifetime of one man, seems stranger than fiction.

SKETCH OF LIFE.

—

CHILDHOOD—ENGAGEMENT WITH AMERICAN FUR CO.— MACKINAW.

I was born in Windsor, Vermont, August 22, 1802. My father was Elizur Hubbard, the son of George Hubbard, an officer in the war of the Revolution, and Thankful Hatch. My mother was Abigal Sage, daughter of General Comfort Sage and Sarah Hamlin, of Middletown, Connecticut.

My first recollection of events was the great eclipse of the sun about the year 1806, while walking with my mother in the garden. The impression made upon my mind by the strange and unnatural appearance of things has lasted to the present time. The white stage horses that were passing, to my vision appeared yellow, and looking up to my mother I discovered that her face also appeared yellow, as did all the surroundings. I was so frightened I did not recover from it for some time.

I cannot remember at what age I commenced going to school, but the fact of a dislike for books, from that time up to the age of thirteen, I do not forget. I was always pleading to be excused, and my indulgent mother too often granted my request. I was often truant and escaped punishment.

My father was, by profession, a lawyer, but having entered into some speculations about the year 1810, in

(5)

the fall of 1812 he lost his property, and my Aunt Saltonstall invited me to her house, and influenced her son-in-law, the Rev. Daniel Huntington, to take me and a boy of about my age to educate.

Accordingly, in November of that year, I went to Bridgewater, Massachusetts, and entered upon a course of studies, living in Mr. Huntington's family, where my aunt also resided.

I was very deficient in my education, but the winter passed pleasantly and I made fair progress in my studies.

My father's misfortunes continued, and he became very poor, which I felt so keenly as to make me miserable and discontented. I constantly pleaded to be permitted to return home, and when, in the following winter, I learned that my father had fallen into still deeper trouble and had determined to go to Montreal, there to practice his profession, I was inconsolable ; and as I had lost all interest in my studies, I was promised that I should return home in the spring.

In the middle of the month of April following I started for my home, and a few days' travel by coach brought me to my parents, and about the first of May, 1815, they, with their six children, of whom I was the eldest, started for Canada. On reaching Montreal, my father learned that he could not be admitted to practice, as he was an American citizen, and by a new law of the Dominion a residence of five years would be required before he could be allowed to practice his profession. He, however, took a house and kept boarders, by which, with the fees he earned as consulting attorney, he received enough to barely support his family, never having a cent to spare beyond their necessary wants.

My first winter there I employed in small traffic, buying from Vermont farmers the remnants of their loads of poultry, butter, cheese, etc., and peddling them, from which I realized from eighty to one hundred dollars, all of which went into the family treasury. The capital with which I embarked in this enterprise was twenty-five cents, and was kindly loaned me by Horatio Gates.

In the month of April, 1816, my father procured for me a situation in the hardware store of John Frothingham, where I received for my services my board only. I was the boy of the store—slept on the counter, worked hard, and attended faithfully to my duties, and thus won the good will of all the clerks. I had but one intimate friend outside of the store, named John Dyde, whom I occasionally visited evenings. His father kept a boarding-house, where Mr. William Matthews, agent of the American Fur Company, boarded.

Mr. John Jacob Astor about this time instructed Mr. Matthews to engage twelve young men as clerks, and one hundred Canadian voyagers, and to purchase a quantity of goods for the Indian trade, to be transferred in *batteaux* manned by these voyagers, and to report therewith to Ramsey Crooks, manager at Mackinaw, Michigan. This expedition was to leave Montreal early in May, 1818, and to proceed as rapidly as possible to its place of destination.

Visiting my friend Dyde one evening, he told me of this, and that he was trying to prevail upon his father and mother to procure for him an engagement with the Fur Company as one of the twelve clerks. He being then but eighteen years old, his parents opposed it on account of his youth, and Mr. Matthews also discouraged the idea; yet he continued his efforts, and finally obtained their consent, and informed me of his good fortune.

The expedition was the subject of frequent conversations between us, and I also became desirous of being employed; my disposition to go increased each time we met, and I finally ventured to mention the subject to my father and mother, but they only laughed at the idea, saying Mr. Matthews would not engage John, as he wanted men, and not boys; that John was not eighteen and I not sixteen. And though I was thus put off, I was not wholly discouraged.

Time passed on and April was near at hand. One morning John came into the store, his countenance beaming with joy, and announced that Mr. Matthews had promised to take him. "Oh!" said he, "I wish you could go with me, but it is of no use to try. It was hard work to induce Mr. Matthews to take me, because I was not old enough, and besides I am the twelfth, and the youngest by four years. I am to get one hundred dollars advanced to purchase my outfit." I don't know what induced me to make any further effort, but I still felt there was a chance.

I could not help crying, and when West, the oldest clerk, inquired the cause, I told him. "Why, Gurdon," he said, "you don't want to go among the Indians. You could not endure the hardships. What a fool you are to think of it. Don't give it another thought. We all like you here. Stick by us, and rise as you will be sure to. Mr. Frothingham has not a word to say against you. He knows you have done your duty, and in time will advance you. So give up the idea."

Just then Mr. Frothingham came in, and, noticing me,

asked what was the matter. I did not reply, but cried. When West told him, he said I had a foolish notion.

I requested leave of absence for the day and night to go home (my father then living at the foot of the mountain), which he granted. I was not long in reaching home, though it was about three miles.

My father was not at home when I arrived, but I told my story to mother, and I thought she was not as strong in her opposition as formerly. When father came I broached the subject to him, and he said I was crazy. I said, "Crazy or not, I want to go, and will if Mr. Matthews will take me," for which speech I received a reprimand. This, however, did not deter me. I kept on teasing for his permission until he finally said, "If your mother is willing, you can go and see Mr. Matthews." She put me off until morning.

I suppose they had a consultation. Indeed, I know that they concluded that Mr. Matthews would reject me. They both knew him, and had both been to his office that day, where my father was employed in writing articles of agreement for the voyagers to sign. My father knew that Mr. Matthews had his full complement of clerks.

In the morning I received permission from my parents to go and see Mr. Matthews, with the understanding that if he would engage me they would consent to my going.

Now, the question was, how to approach Mr. Matthews, and I formed many plans, but finally, trusting to Mr. Dyde for an introduction, and getting him to get his parents to offer my services and intercede for me on the ground of my friendship for their son, an interview with Mr. Matthews was had. He told me that he had his full complement of clerks and men engaged, and that I was really too young to go; but he finally said to me, "If you can get your parents' consent I will engage you for five years and pay you one hundred and twenty dollars per year, more on account of John Dyde than anything else, as he wants you to go with him." I then knew the negotiation was ended, as I had my father's word, which never failed.

I sought my father and reported, and he and my mother were sorely disappointed and grieved, but offered no further opposition.

The agreement was soon thereafter signed, and I drew fifty dollars which my mother expended for my outfit. A part of my outfit consisted of a swallow-tail coat (the first I ever had) and pants and vest, all of which were much too large for me, and designed to be filled by my future growth.

The clerks were allowed a small wooden chest in which to keep their outfit, for which the company charged them three dollars; the chest and contents weighed about sixty pounds. In one of these my wardrobe was packed, with other necessary articles prepared by my mother.

Every preparation having been made for my departure, I reported myself in readiness.

Orders were issued for the voyagers to report on the 1st of May at Lachine, and the clerks were to report at the same place on the 13th of May, at ten o'clock a. m.

Mr. Wallace, with three or four clerks, was detailed to take charge of the loading of the boats on May 1st.

On the 13th of May, 1818, having bid adieu to my mother and sisters, I started with my father and brother for

Lachine, where I arrived about nine o'clock in the morning and reported for duty.

The boats were all loaded, the clerks and voyagers were there, and many friends and relatives had assembled to bid them farewell; all were strangers to me, except my friend Dyde, Mr. Matthews and Mr. Wallace.

To Mr. Wallace was assigned the duty of arranging the crews, and detailing the clerks to the different boats. Mr. Wallace was a Scotchman, and was one of a party who was sent by Mr. Astor to the Columbia River on an expedition which was broken up by the war of 1812. He, with others, returned overland; their vessel, having been attacked by Indians, was blown up by one of the men on board. He was a man of large experience and of great energy and capacity, and, like most Scotchmen, was a strict disciplinarian, with a powerful will and of undaunted courage.

Though sixty-two years have passed since then, I distinctly remember the animating and affecting scene presented that morning. All being ready for the departure, it was announced that a half-hour would be given for leave-taking, and during that time every man was at liberty and under no restraint. Then came the parting embraces; tears and blessings being showered on all.

Mr. Matthews had embarked in the largest boat, which was gaily decorated, and manned by a picked crew of voyagers.

The time for leave-takings having expired, Mr. Wallace, in a loud voice, gave the command, "To boats all"; and in a few moments all hands were aboard and pushing off from the shore amid cheers and farewell shouts.

The voyagers in Mr. Matthews' boat started the boat song, which was joined in by all the voyagers and clerks in the expedition. Stout arms and brave hearts were at the oars, and the boats fairly flew through the blue waters of the St. Lawrence River.

My friend Dyde and myself had been assigned to the same boat, a favor we recognized as coming from Mr. Matthews.

I cannot describe my feelings as I looked back upon the forms of my father and brother, from whom I was then about to be separated. Nor did I, until that time, realize my situation or regret my engagement. The thought that I might never again see those most dear to me filled my soul with anguish. Bitter tears I could not help shedding, nor did I care to.

When the boats stopped for lunch at noon, the clerks were invited to meet Mr. Matthews, and were then introduced to each other, Mr. Matthews making a short speech to them.

Our lunch consisted of wine, crackers and cheese, and in a half-hour from the time of halting we resumed our journey.

About four o'clock in the afternoon we camped for the night. The clerks all messed with Mr. Matthews, in a mess-tent provided for the purpose. One small sleeping tent was allotted to four clerks.

The men had no shelter except tarpaulins, which, in stormy weather, were placed upon poles, thus forming a roof. Log fires were kindled at either or both ends, and each man was provided with one blanket.

The voyagers kept their clothing and tobacco in linen or tow bags provided by the company for that purpose. The clerks were supplied with a thin mattress, upon which two slept, and a blanket each, and a small tarpaulin in which to roll up their mattress and blankets. The tarpaulin also served as a carpet for the tents.

The men were fed exclusively upon pea soup and salt pork, and on Sunday an extra allowance of hard biscuit. The tables of the clerks were also supplied with salt pork and pea soup, and in addition thereto, with tea, sugar, hard bread, and such meats as could be procured from time to time.

All took breakfast at daybreak, and soon after sunrise the boats were under way. One hour was allowed at noon for dinner, and at sundown we camped for the night, which made a long day of hard work for the men, though they were occasionally allowed ten minutes " to pipe," *i. e.*, to fill their pipes for smoking.

Our boats were heavily laden, and our progress up the swift St. Lawrence was necessarily slow. Some days, when we had "rapids" to overcome, three to five miles was the full day's journey. And where the rapids were heavy, the crews of three, and sometimes four boats were allotted to one, seven or eight of the men being in the water, pushing and pulling and keeping the boat from sheering into the current.

Two men remained in the boat, one in the bow, the other at the stern, with iron-pointed poles to aid the men in the water, and to steer and keep her bow heading the current, the rest of the men on the shore pulling on a rope which was attached to the bow. Yet with all this force, the current at times was so strong the boat would scarcely move; and the force of the current would raise the water to the very top of the "cut-water," and sometimes even over the sides of the boat.

On several occasions, the boat and men were dragged

back until they found an "eddy," when all would stop
and rest for another effort   This work was very severe
on the men, they toiling from early morning until night,
with only an hour's interval at noon, and an occasional
respite while stemming a swift current.

Great dissatisfaction prevailed among the voyagers,
and, desertions becoming frequent, guards were established at night, consisting of the clerks; and yet scarcely
a morning appeared that some were not missing. We,
however, moved steadily along, making a daily average
of about fifteen miles, we clerks, sauntering, whenever
inclination led us, on the banks, or sometimes inland for
several miles, stopping at houses occasionally and chatting with the inmates, where we were always cordially
received, and often treated to the best they had. The
news of the advancing brigade preceded us, and we found
them fully posted as to our coming. At one time we
received a pleasant visit from the late Hiram Norton, of
Lockport, Illinois, who then resided on the St. Lawrence;
and then began an acquaintance which in later years
ripened into a warm friendship.

Notwithstanding these excursions and the beauty and
variety of the scenery through which we passed, our
daily routine became extremely monotonous. We were
about a month in reaching Toronto, then called "Little
York," a small town of about three hundred inhabitants,
mostly Canadian French. By this time the number of
our men was greatly reduced by desertions, and Mr.
Matthews began to fear that he would be obliged to leave
some of the boats for want of crews. The hard work,
however, was over, as from that point there was no more
current to hinder our progress. Here Mr. Matthews

changed our route, and instead of passing through Lake Erie via Buffalo, as was intended, he hired ox teams, loading our goods in carts, and detailing most of the clerks to accompany them over to what was called "Youngs Street," to Lake Simcoe, where we encamped and remained some two weeks, until all our boats were hauled over and launched into that romantic little lake and reloaded. Two yoke of cattle were also put on board one of the boats. We struck camp and proceeded to the other end, where the goods and boats, with the help of the oxen, made the Not-ta-wa-sa-ga portage, into the river of the same name. Though this portage was only six miles, we were a week conveying our goods and boats across. During this time we were nearly devoured with mosquitos and gnats. We were in an uninhabited wilderness, with no road over the low swamp lands. Desertion among the men had ceased, for the very good reason that there was no chance to escape. All rejoiced when we were again in our boats, and, with the current aiding us, swept down the winding course of the Nottawasaga River. The worst of the journey was now over, and with lightened hearts the voyagers again lifted their voices and joined in the melodious boat songs. We descended the river to Lake Huron, which we coasted.

Early in the afternoon of the third of July we reached Goose Island, and camped in sight of Mich il-i-mac-i-nac, "The Great Turtle," the wind being too strong from the west to admit of our crossing the open lake. However, as the island abounded in gull's eggs, we spent an agreeable evening around our camp fires, feasting on them.

As the lake was still rough, the morning of the fourth being too stormy to venture across, we devoted the time

to washing, and dressing in our best clothing, not so
much in commemoration of the day, as of our joy at
the sight of that beautiful island where our wearisome
voyage was to end, thankful that we had been brought
in safety, without accident, through so many difficulties
and perils. We became so impatient at the delay that
about two o'clock in the afternoon we started across, but
the wind continued so high that the passage took about
three hours, and we were unable to round the point of
the island, but were compelled to land on the east side,
at the foot of " Robinson's Folly."

Here we were met by Messrs. Ramsey Crooks and
Robert Stewart, the managers of the American Fur
Company, together with a host of clerks and voyagers,
who extended to us a cordial welcome, and thus we
celebrated the fourth of July, 1818.

On this island lived old voyagers, worn out with the
hard service incident to their calling, with their families
of half-breeds.

A few, only, of the inhabitants engaged in trade. Mrs.
Mitchell, an energetic, enterprising woman, the wife
of Dr. Mitchell, a surgeon of the English army,
and stationed at Drummond's Island, had a store and
small farm. Michael Dousman, Edward Biddle, and
John Drew were also merchants, all depending on trading
with the Indians.

These merchants, to a very great extent, were under
the influence of the American Fur Company, purchasing
most of their goods from them, and selling to them their
furs and peltries. This island was the headquarters of
the American Fur Company, and here I first learned
something of the working and discipline of that mam

moth corporation, and took my first lessons in the life of an Indian trader, a life which I followed exclusively for ten consecutive years. Here, also, was located Fort Mackinaw, at that time garrisoned by three or four companies of United States troops. The village had a population of about five hundred, mostly of Canadian French and of mixed Indian blood, whose chief occupation was fishing in summer and hunting in winter. There were not more than twelve white women on the island, the residue of the female population being either all or part Indian. Here, during the summer months, congregated the traders employed by the Fur Company, bringing their collections from their several trading posts, which extended from the British dominions on the north and the Missouri River in the west, south and east to the white settlements; in fact, to all the Indian hunting grounds, so that when all were collected they added three thousand or more to the population.

The Indians from the shores of the upper lakes, who made this island a place of resort, numbered from two to three thousand more. Their wigwams lined the entire beach two or three rows deep, and, with the tents of the traders, made the island a scene of life and animation. The voyageurs were fond of fun and frolic, and the Indians indulged in their love of liquor, and, by the exhibition of their war, medicine, and other dances and sports, often made both night and day hideous with their yells. These *voyageurs* were all Canadian French, and were the only people fitted for the life they were compelled to endure, their cheerful temperament and happy disposition making them contented under the privations and hardships incident to their calling.

At the time of our arrival, all the traders from the North and the Great West had reached the island with their returns of furs collected from the Indians during the previous winter, which were being counted and appraised, and the profit or loss of each "outfit" ascertained.

All of the different outfits were received into a large warehouse, where they were assorted into various classes or grades, carefully counted, packed, and pressed for shipment to New York to John Jacob Astor, the president of the company.

The work of assorting required expert judges of furs, a nice discrimination between the different grades being necessary, as prices varied very greatly, there being as many as six grades. Marten (sable), for example, being classed as extra fine dark, number one dark, number two dark, number one fine brown, number two fine brown, number one fine, common, number two common, number three common, good, out of season, inferior, damaged, and worthless. The value of the fur of this animal depended as much on color as fineness, and was found in the greatest variety of shades of color, and, with the exception of silver gray fox, was the most valuable. Mink, muskrat, raccoon, lynx, wild cat, fox, wolverine, badger, otter, beaver, and other small fur animals, received the same care, except there were fewer grades of quality. In bear skins, only, were there more than four grades, but in those the discrimination was nearly equal to marten, being extra fine black *she*, number two ditto, fine number one, number two ditto, and fine, coarse, and numbers one, two, and three *he bear*. Deer skins required but little skill in assorting; they were classed as red doe, red buck, blue doe, blue buck, season doe, season buck, out of season, and damaged.

The commanders of outfits were deeply interested in the assortment of their furs, and were very watchful to see that justice was done them; for upon this depended their balance sheets of profit or loss. Hence, frequent disputes arose as to the grade and value of the skins.

Mr. Matthews had the general management of the fur warehouse, and on arrival assumed the charge. After a few days I was ordered to report to him, and then commenced my first instructions in the fur trade.

It was my business to make a second count in order to verify the first. The first count was entered on a book not seen by me, and if mine corresponded with it, the furs were placed in a frame, pressed, marked, and rolled into the shipping wareroom. If, however, my count did not agree with the first, I was required to make a second count, and if there was still a discrepancy, a third person was called upon to recount them. This work took about two months, the working hours being from five o'clock in the morning to twelve noon, and from one to seven in the afternoon, and, as I was obliged to maintain a stooping posture, was severely fatiguing.

About one hundred voyageurs were detailed to assist in this business, and were kept under strict discipline. Most of them were experienced, and were generally contented and happy, each working with a will, knowing that Mackinaw fatigue duty came but once in four years, and that if they lived through the succeeding three years, their time at headquarters could be spent in comparative ease and comfort.

A party was also organized to cut wood on Bois

Blanc, and bring it in boats to the island for the use of the agents and employés who remained there: this party consisted of about twenty-five picked choppers, under the charge of one of the clerks detailed for that purpose. Another party was employed in lyeing (hulling) corn, and drying and putting up for the use of those remaining on the island, and for supplying the various outfits soon to leave for their trading posts.

The daily ration issued by the commissary to a mess of from six to ten men, consisted of one pint of lyed or hulled and dried corn, with from two to four ounces of tallow, to each man ; and this was all the food they received, except that on Saturday flour was given them for Sunday pancakes. It would seem that this was a very short and light ration for healthy, hard-working men, but it was quite sufficient, and generally more than they could consume. It was invariably liked by them, and it was found that they could endure more hardships on this than on a diet of bread and meat.

Those who came from Canada, their first season, and who were called *mangé-du-lard*, or "pork-eaters," were usually much dissatisfied and angered with this ration, as on the voyage up they were fed on pork, pease, and hard bread, and the change was anything but agreeable to them. They were, however, soon laughed out of it by the old voyageurs, who told them that many of them would be thankful for even that before they returned from their winter quarters.

The Company had a yard in which were made and repaired their own boats, and where were manufactured traps, tomahawks, and other articles from iron. Other parties of the men were detailed to assist the mechanics in this work.

Most of the clerks were assigned to duty either in charge of the different gangs of men or in the wholesale and retail stores and offices. From these duties the heads of outfits were exempt.

The force of the Company, when all were assembled on the island, comprised about four hundred clerks and traders, together with some two thousand voyageurs. About five hundred of these were quartered in barracks, one hundred lived in the agency house, and the others were camped in tents and accommodated in rooms of the Islanders.

Dances and parties were given every night by the residents of the island in honor of the traders, and they, in their turn, reciprocated with balls and jollifications, which, though not as elegant and costly as those of the present day, were sufficiently so to drain from the participants all the hard earnings of the winter previous.

In each "brigade," or outfit, was to be found one who, from superior strength or bravery, was looked upon as the "bully" of that crew of voyageurs, and who, as a distinguishing mark, wore a black feather in his cap.

These "bullies" were generally good fighters, and were always governed by the rules of fair play. It was a rule, and was expected, that they should fight each other; hence it was not an uncommon thing to see a fight. The vanquished one gave up his black feather to the conqueror, or shook hands with him, and they both joined with the lookers on in a glass of beer or whisky as good-naturedly as though nothing unpleasant had occurred.

The majority of the inhabitants of the island were of

mixed blood—Canadian and Indian—and those who were of pure blood, and were heads of families, had Indian wives. Their children, though uneducated, were usually bright and intelligent, and fond of finery, dancing, and other amusements. There were a few of the half-breeds who had received a common education, either in English or French, which was generally of little use to them, as they were mostly too lazy or proud to earn a livelihood.

Among the Indian or part Indian women who were, or had been, married to white husbands, were found some of great intellectual capacity, who carried on an extensive trade with the Indians, one of whom was the Mrs. Mitchell before referred to; she had a store and a farm, both under excellent management, and her children had been well educated in Canada. This woman's husband was a Scotchman and a surgeon in the English army, and while the Island of Mackinaw was in the possession of England he was stationed there; removing afterwards to Drummond's Island, he rarely visited his family, though only fifty miles distant. He was a man of strong prejudices, hated the "Yankees," and would hold no social intercourse with them.

Mrs. Mitchell was quite the reverse, and being rather partial to the "Yankees," treated them with great consideration: she was a fine housekeeper and owned one of the best houses on the island; she was fond of good society, very hospitable, and entertained handsomely, conversing in French and English, both of which she spoke fluently.

Another of these women was Mrs. Lafromboise, who also traded with the Indians in the interior, usually up the Grand River of Michigan; her daughter was highly educated, and married the commanding officer at Fort Mackinaw.

Mrs. Lafromboise could read and write, and was a perfect lady in her manners and conversation; she was a widow, her husband, who was a trader, having been shot and killed by an Indian on the Mississippi River; she took his place and business and accumulated considerable money. She was afterwards employed on a salary by the American Fur Company.

Mrs. Chandler, a sister of Mrs. Lafromboise, was also noted for her ladylike manners and many Christian virtues. Her husband was an invalid and her daughter a widow. This daughter was also highly educated and was considered the belle of Mackinaw; she afterwards married Mr. Beard, a lawyer of Green Bay, Wisconsin.

It was my good fortune to be received into these excellent families as a welcome visitor, and they all took an interest in me and my welfare, calling me their "boy clerk." My leisure evenings were passed with them, much to my pleasure and advantage. From them I received much good advice, as well as instruction in the method of conducting trade with the Indians, which was of much benefit to me in my after life as a trader.

It was also my good fortune to form the acquaintance of Mr. Deschamps, who was an old man and the head of the "Illinois outfit."

Mr. Deschamps had been educated at Quebec for a Roman Catholic priest, but, refusing to be ordained, he, at the age of nineteen, engaged himself to Mr. Sara, a fur trader at St. Louis, and had devoted many years of his life to the Indian trade on the Ohio and Illinois Rivers. When the American Fur Company was organized he was engagd by them and placed in charge of the "Illinois brigade," or outfit.

It was the policy of the American Fur Company to monopolize the entire fur trade of the Northwest; and to this end they engaged fully nineteen-twentieths of all the traders of that territory, and with their immense capital and influence succeeded in breaking up the business of any trader who refused to enter their service.

Very soon after reaching Mackinaw and making returns, the traders commenced organizing their crews and preparing their outfits for their return to winter quarters at their various trading posts, those destined for the extreme North being the first to receive attention. These outfits were called "brigades."

The "brigade" destined for the Lake of the Woods, having the longest journey to make, was the first to depart. They were transported in boats called "batteaux," which very much resembled the boats now used by fishermen on the great lakes, except that they were larger, and were each manned by a crew of five men besides a clerk. Four of the men rowed while the fifth steered. Each boat carried about three tons of merchandise, together with the clothing of the men and rations of corn and tallow. No shelter was provided for the voyageurs, and their luggage was confined to twenty pounds in weight, carried in a bag provided for that purpose.

The commander of the "brigade" took for his own use the best boat, and with him an extra man, who acted in the capacity of "orderly" to the expedition, and the *will* of the commander was the only law known.

The clerks were furnished with salt pork, a bag of flour,

tea and coffee, and a tent for shelter, and messed with the commander and orderly.

A vast multitude assembled at the harbor to witness their departure, and when all was ready the boats glided from the shore, the crews singing some favorite boat song, while the multitude shouted their farewells and wishes for a successful trip and a safe return; and thus outfit after outfit started on its way for Lake Superior, Upper and Lower Mississippi, and other posts.

The "Wabash and Illinois River outfits" were almost the last, and were speedily followed by the smaller ones for the shores of Lakes Huron and Michigan, and which consisted of but from one to three boats.

I was detailed to the Fond-du-Lac (Lake Superior) "brigade," and a week or so before its departure was relieved from duty at the fur warehouse.

About this time I received a letter from my father, written at Erie, Pennsylvania, in which he informed me that he and my brother were there on their way to St. Louis, and that they had waited there a week looking for the Fur Company's vessel, which it was expected would touch there on her way from Buffalo to Mackinaw, upon which they hoped to obtain passage, and thus visit me, and if they found no way of proceeding to St. Louis from there, they would return on the vessel to Erie; but fearing she had passed, and being uncertain whether they should find me on the island, they had reluctantly concluded to continue their journey by way of Cincinnati.

I had before this been told by Mr. Deschamps that he made a trip every fall to St. Louis, with one boat, to purchase supplies of tobacco and other necessaries for distribution among the various traders on the Illinois

River; and as he had seemed fond of me, and possessed my confidence, I went immediately to him with my letter, thinking to advise with him, and, perhaps, to send by him an answer to my father. After hearing my story, he delighted me by saying, "Would you like to go with me, if it can be so arranged?" to which I answered affirmatively, and begged for his influence and efforts to that end.

A Mr. Warner, a fellow clerk from Montreal, had been detailed to Mr. Deschamps' "brigade."

"Now," said Mr. Deschamps, "if you can get Mr. Warner to consent to an exchange, I think I can get Mr. Crooks' permission; I can see no objection to it, and as I am the party mostly interested, I think it can be arranged with him: you must first, however, obtain Mr. Warner's consent, and then I will see what I can do."

So off I started, letter in hand, to see Warner, not daring to hope for success; but to my surprise I found he preferred going north to south, and would gladly make the change. I reported to Mr. Deschamps, and he, seeing my anxiety, took my letter and went immediately to Mr. Crooks, who gave his consent, and with it an order to the book-keeper to change the names in the details; you may feel certain that I felt much rejoiced at my good fortune. Thus my desire of finding my father in St. Louis was the probable cause of an entire change in my destiny, for, instead of being located in the cold regions of the North where my friend Warner froze to death that winter, my lot was cast in this beautiful State.

During my stay at Mackinaw I had made the acquaintance of John H. Kinzie, a clerk of about my own age, and our acquaintance had ripened into an intimacy. He had entered the service of the company that spring, and was stationed permanently at Mackinaw, and was not to be sent into the Indian country. His father then resided at Chicago, and I had learned of the great hospitality of the family, and of the high esteem felt for them by all who knew them; and as I had also been told that we should make a stop of a week or more at Chicago, there to make our arrangements for crossing our boats and goods to the Desplaines River, I gladly accepted letters of introduction which he kindly proffered me, to his father and family.

Through my intimacy with John I had become quite familiar with the appearance of the Kinzie family and their surroundings. I knew that Fort Dearborn was located at Chicago, then a frontier post; that it was garrisoned by two companies of soldiers, and that on my arrival there I should for the first time in my life see a prairie; and I felt that my new detail was to take me among those who would be my friends, and was happy in the thought.

The time of our departure soon arrived, and about noon on the 10th of September, 1818, our "brigade" left the harbor in twelve boats.

Mr. Deschamps took me in his boat, and led the way, with his fine, strong voice starting the boat song, in which all the crews heartily joined.

The people on the shore bid us a "God speed," and joined with us in the hope for our safe return the next season.

The Islanders, more than any one else, regretted our departure, as what few of the traders remained would go in a few days and leave them to the monotony of their own surroundings, even the Indians having mostly departed for their hunting grounds.

Some of our boats were crowded with the families of the traders, the oldest of whom was Mr. Bieson, a large, portly, gray-headed man, who was then about sixty years of age, and for more than forty years had been an Indian trader on the Ohio, Mississippi, and Illinois Rivers. His wife was a pure-blooded Pottawatomie Indian, enormous in size—so fleshy she could scarcely walk. Their two daughters were married, and lived at Cahokie, a small French town opposite St. Louis. Mr. Bieson had a house and some property at Opa (now Peoria), but had been, with all the inhabitants of that place, driven off by the United States troops, under command of General Howard, in the year 1813, and a fort was there erected, which was called Fort Clark. The town of Opa and Fort Clark were situated at the foot of Lake Peoria, on the Illinois River, where now stands the flourishing city of Peoria.

The inhabitants of Opa were suspected (wrongly, I think) by our government of being enemies, and of aiding and counseling the Indians in giving assistance to Great Britain, and this was the cause of General Howard's action in compelling them to vacate. Undoubtedly some of them favored the British, and was paid spies, but a large majority opposed the Indians in siding with the British, and counseled them to act neutrally and attend to their hunting.

Among the others, who had with them their families, were Messrs. Bebeau, of Opa, and Lefrombois, Bleau, and La Clare, all of whom had Indian wives; and, in fact, there were but three or four single men in the party. Those having families messed by themselves, while the single men clubbed together. Mr. Deschamps was fond of good living, and our mess of five was well provided for, having such meats, fish, and wild fruits as were presented to us by the Indians when we met them on the shore of Lake Michigan.

It was a custom of the Indians to present the head man of an expedition with the best they had, expecting to receive in return, salt, powder, or something else of value to them. The choice parts were retained by Mr. Deschamps for his own table, and the balance distributed among the traders.

The traders were all provided with small tents, but the only shelter given to the men was what was afforded by the boat tarpaulins, and, indeed, no other was needed, the camp fires being sufficient for warmth during the night. No covering but their single blanket was required, unless the weather was stormy.

The boats progressed at the rate of about forty miles per day under oars, and when the wind was fair we hoisted our square sails, by the aid of which we were enabled to make seventy or seventy-five miles per day. If the wind proved too heavy, or blew strong ahead, we sought an entrance into the first creek or river we came to, and there awaited a favorable time to proceed. If caught by a storm on the coast, when a shelter could not be reached, we sought the shore, where our boats were unloaded and hauled up on to the beach out of reach of the surf. This was a hard and fatiguing labor, and was accomplished by laying down poles on the sand from the edge of the water. The men then waded into the water on each side of the boat, and by lifting and pushing as each large wave rolled against it, finally succeeded in landing it high and dry on the shore. The goods were then piled up, resting on poles, and covered over with the tarpaulins, which were raised to the leeward by poles, so as to form a good shelter for the men and protect them from wind and rain. Sometimes we were compelled to remain thus in camp for four or five days at a time, waiting for the storm to subside, and during this time many games were indulged in, such as racing, wrestling, and card playing, and all were jolly and contented; sometimes varying the monotony by hunting or fishing.

Our journey around Lake Michigan was rather a long one, having occupied about twenty days. Nothing of interest transpired until we reached Marquette River.

about where the town of Ludington now stands. This was the spot where Father Marquette died, about one hundred and forty years before, and we saw the remains of a red-cedar cross, erected by his men at the time of his death to mark his grave; and though his remains had been removed to the Mission, at Point St. Ignace, the cross was held sacred by the voyageurs, who, in passing, paid reverence to it by kneeling and making the sign of the cross. It was about three feet above the ground, and in a falling condition. We re-set it, leaving it out of the ground about two feet, and as I never saw it after, I doubt not that it was covered by the drifting sands of the following winter, and that no white man ever saw it afterwards.

We proceeded on our voyage, and on the evening of September 30, 1818, reached the mouth of the Calumet River, then known as the " Little Calumet," where we met a party of Indians returning to their villages from a visit to Chicago. They were very drunk, and before midnight commenced a fight in which several of their number were killed. Owing to this disturbance we removed our camp to the opposite side of the river and spent the remainder of the night in dressing ourselves and preparing for our advent into Chicago.

We started at dawn. The morning was calm and bright, and we, in our holiday attire, with flags flying, completed the last twelve miles of our lake voyage. Arriving at Douglas Grove, where the prairie could be seen through the oak woods, I landed, and climbing a tree, gazed in admiration on the first prairie I had ever seen. The waving grass, intermingling with a rich profusion of wild flowers, was the most beautiful sight I had ever gazed upon. In the distance the grove of Blue Island loomed up, beyond it the timber on the Desplaines River, while to give animation to the scene, a herd of wild deer appeared, and a pair of red foxes emerged from the grass within gunshot of me.

Looking north, I saw the whitewashed buildings of Fort Dearborn sparkling in the sunshine, our boats with flags flying, and oars keeping time to the cheering boat-song. I was spell-bound and amazed at the beautiful scene befor me. I took the trail leading to the fort, and, on my arrival, found our party camped on the north side of the river, near what is now State street. A soldier ferried me across the river in a canoe, and thus I made my first entry into Chicago, October 1, 1818.

We were met upon landing by Mr. Kinzie, and as soon as our tents were pitched, were called upon by the officers of the fort, to all of whom I was introduced by Mr. Deschamps as his boy. I presented my letter of introduction to Mr. Kinzie, and with it a package sent by his son. In the afternoon I called at Mr. Kinzie's house, and had the pleasure of meeting his family—consisting of Mrs. Kinzie; their eldest daughter, Mrs. Helm; their youngest daughter, Maria, now the wife of Major-General David Hunter, of the U. S. Army, and their youngest son, Robert, late paymaster of the U. S. Army, all of whom extended to me a cordial welcome. As I had so recently seen John, and had been so intimate with him, I had much of interest to tell them.

I was invited to breakfast with them the next morning, and gladly accepted. As I sat down to the neat and well-ordered table for the first time since I left my father's house, memories of home and those dear to me forced themselves upon me, and I could not suppress my tears. But for the kindness of Mrs. Kinzie I should have beaten a hasty retreat. She saw my predicament and said, " I know just how you feel, and know more about you than you think ; I am going to be a mother to you if you will let me. Just come with me a moment." She led me into an adjoining room and left me to bathe my eyes in cold water. When I came to the table I noticed that they had suspended eating, awaiting my return. I said to Mrs. Kinzie, " You reminded me so much of my mother, I could not help crying ; my last meal with her was when I left Montreal, and since then I have never sat at a table with ladies, and this seems like home to me." Mr. Kinzie's house was a long log cabin, with a rude piazza, and fronted the river directly opposite Fort Dearborn.

FORT DEARBORN.

Fort Dearborn was first established in 1804, on the south bank of Chicago River near where it then discharged into lake Michigan.

It was evacuated August 15, 1812, by Capt. N. Heald, 1st U. S. Infantry, who was then in command, and it was on the same day destroyed by the Indians.

It was rebuilt on the old site in June, 1816, by Capt. Hezekiah Bradley, 3d U. S. Infantry, and occupied by troops until October, 1823, when it was again vacated and left in charge of Alexander Wolcott, Indian Agent.

Re-occupied, October 3, 1828.

Troops again withdrawn, May 20, 1831.

Re-occupied, June 17, 1832.

Again vacated, July 11, 1832.

Re-occupied, October 1, 1832.

And finally abandoned, December 29, 1836.

I have been unable to find from the records of the War Department by whom this post was originally established, but find it to have been commanded, after its re-establishment, by officers as follows:

Capt. Hezekiah Bradley, 3d U. S. Infantry, from June, 1816, to May, 1817.

Brev. Maj. D. Baker, 3d U. S. Infantry, to June, 1820.

Capt. H. Bradley, 3d U. S. Infantry, to January, 1821.

Maj. Alexander Cummings, 3d U. S. Infantry, to October, 1822.

Lieut.-Col. McNeil, 3d U. S. Infantry, to October, 1823.

Fort not garrisoned from October, 1823, to October 3, 1828.

Capt. John Fowle, 5th U. S. Infantry, from October 3, 1828, to December 21, 1830.

Lieut. David Hunter, 5th U. S. Infantry, to May 20, 1831, when the troops were withdrawn.

Maj. William Whistler, 2d U. S. Infantry, from June 17, 1832, to July 11, 1832, and from October 1, 1832, to June 19, 1833.

When I first saw Fort Dearborn it was a stockade of oak pickets fourteen feet long, inclosing a square of about six hundred feet.

A block house stood at the southwest corner, and a bastion in the northwest corner, about a hundred feet from which was the river.

In the first fort an underground passage was constructed from the bastion to the river's edge, but this was not kept open during the occupancy of the second, but was kept in condition to be speedily re-opened should occasion ever require it.

The officers' quarters were outside of the pickets, fronting east on the parade, and was a two-story building of hewn logs. A piazza extended along the entire front on a line with the floor of the second story, and was reached by stairs on the outside.

The first story was divided into kitchen, dining and store rooms, while the second story was in one large room. The roof was covered with split clapboards about four feet long.

The soldiers' quarters were also of logs, and similar to the officers', except that both stories were finished off and divided into rooms.

In the northeast corner was the sutler's store, also built of logs, while at the north and south sides were gates opening to the parade ground.

On each side of the south gate were guardhouses, about ten feet square.

The commissary storehouse was two stories in height, and stood east of the guardhouse and south of the soldiers' quarters.

The magazine was constructed of brick, and was situated west of the guardhouse, and near the block house. The stockade and all the buildings were neatly whitewashed, and presented a neat and pleasing appearance.

West, and a little south, of the fort was the military barn, adjoining which, on the east, was the fort garden, of about four acres, which extended so as to front the fort on the south, its eastern line of fence connecting with and forming a part of the *field* extending south about half a mile.

Adjoining this fence on the east was the only road leading from the fort in either direction. The south line of the garden fence extended to the edge of the river, and a fence from the west end of the barn extended north to the river, so that the fort was wholly inclosed by fence from river to river. The inclosure between the stockade and the outer fences was covered with grass and adorned with trees and shrubbery.

The well was in the outer inclosure and near the south gate, while about two hundred feet from the north gate was the river, a stream of clear, pure water, fed from the lake.

On the east side of the fort the river was from four to five hundred feet from the pickets, and a part of this distance was a low, sandy beach, where rude wash-houses had been constructed, in which the men and women of the garrison conducted their laundry operations.

Just east of the road, and adjoining the fence running east to the river, was the "Factor House," a two-story, squared-log structure, inclosed by a neat split-picket fence. This building was occupied from 1804 to about the year 1810 by a Mr. Jonett, United States factor, and by the west side of the road, adjoining the government garden, in a picket-fence inclosure, was the grave of his wife. At the second construction of the fort he was succeeded by John Dean.

For a distance of a quarter of a mile from the "Factor House" there was no fence, building, or other obstruction between the government-field fence and the river or lake. Another house of hewn logs stood twelve hundred or more feet from the road, and back of it flowed the Chicago River, which, as late as 1827, emptied into Lake

Michigan at a point known as "The Pines," a clump of a hundred or more stunted pine trees on the sand-hills about a mile from the fort. On the edge of the river, directly east of this house, and distant about four hundred feet, stood a storehouse of round logs, owned by the American Fur Company and occupied by its agent, Mr. John Craft, who erected it. This house was surrounded by a rail fence, and, after the death of Mr. Craft, was occupied by Jean Baptiste Beaubien.

Adjoining this storehouse on the south was the fort burying-ground. The east line of the government field extended to about this point, and thence west to the south branch of the river. These, with the addition of a log cabin near the present Bridgeport, called "Hard-scrabble," a cabin on the north side occupied by Antoine Ouilmette, and the house of Mr. Kinzie, comprised all the buildings within the present limits of Cook County.

Between the river and the lake, and extending south to "The Pines," was a narrow strip of sand formed by the northeast winds gradually forcing the mouth of the river south of its natural and original outlet at Fort Dearborn.

In the spring of 1828, the Chicago River had a strong current caused by flood; and, taking advantage of this, the officer commanding at the fort ordered some of his men to cut a passage through the spit of land at the commencement of the bend and parallel with the north side of the fort. It was the work of but an hour or two to dig a ditch down to the level of the river, and the water being let in, the force of the current soon washed a straight channel through to the lake fifteen or more feet deep ; but the ever-shifting sand soon again filled this channel, and the mouth of the river worked south to about where Madison street now is.

To Captain Fowle, however, are we indebted for the first attempt to make a harbor of the Chicago River.

The officers amused themselves with fishing and hunting; deer, red fox, and wild-fowl were abundant. Foxes burrowed in the sand-hills and were often dug out, brought to the fort, and let loose upon the sand-bar formed by the outlet of the river. They were then chased by hounds, men being stationed so as to prevent their escape from the bar. These fox hunts were very exciting, and were enjoyed by Indians and whites alike. None of the officers were married, and as the suttler's store furnished the only means of spending their money they were forced to be frugal and saving. They were a convivial, jolly set.

Fort Wayne, Indiana, was the nearest post-office, and the mail was carried generally by soldiers on foot and was received once a month. The wild onion grew in great quantities along the banks of the river, and in the woods adjoining, the leek abounded, and doubtless Chicago derived its name from the onion and not, as some suppose, from the (animal) skunk. The Indian name for this animal is chi-kack, for the vegetable, chi-goug; both words were used to indicate strong odors.

What is now known as the North Branch was then known as River Guarie, named after the first trader that followed La Salle. The field he cultivated was traceable on the prairie by the distinct marks of the cornhills.

After a few days at Chicago, spent in repairing our boats, we struck camp and proceeded up the lagoon, or what is now known as the South Branch, camping at a point near the present commencement of the Illinois and Michigan Canal, where we remained one day preparing to pass our boats through Mud Lake into the Aux Plaines River.

Mud Lake drained partly into the Aux Plaines and partly through a narrow, crooked channel into the South Branch, and only in very wet seasons was there sufficient water to float an empty boat. The mud was very deep, and along the edge of the lake grew tall grass and wild rice, often reaching above a man's head, and so strong and dense it was almost impossible to walk through them.

Our empty boats were pulled up the channel, and in many places, where there was no water and a hard clay bottom, they were placed on short rollers, and in this way moved along until the lake was reached, where we found mud thick and deep, but only at rare intervals was there water. Forked tree branches were tied upon

(39)

the ends of the boat poles, and these afforded a bearing on the tussocks of grass and roots, which enabled the men in the boat to push to some purpose. Four men only remained in a boat and pushed with these poles, while six or eight others waded in the mud alongside, and by united efforts constantly jerking it along, so that from early dawn to dark we succeeded only in passing a part of our boats through to the Aux Plaines outlet, where we found the first hard ground. While a part of our crew were thus employed, others busied themselves in transporting our goods on their backs to the river; it was a laborious day for all.

Those who waded through the mud frequently sank to their waist, and at times were forced to cling to the side of the boat to prevent going over their heads; after reaching the end and camping for the night came the task of ridding themselves from the blood suckers.

The lake was full of these abominable black plagues, and they stuck so tight to the skin that they broke in pieces if force was used to remove them; experience had taught the use of a decoction of tobacco to remove them, and this was resorted to with good success.

Having rid ourselves of the blood suckers, we were assailed by myriads of mosquitoes, that rendered sleep hopeless, though we sought the softest spots on the ground for our beds.

Those who had waded the lake suffered great agony, their limbs becoming swollen and inflamed, and their sufferings were not ended for two or three days.

It took us three consecutive days of such toil to pass all our boats through this miserable lake; when we finally camped on the banks of the river, our goods had all crossed the portage and we were once more ready to proceed.

Our boats being again loaded, we resumed our voyage down the Desplaines until we reached Isle La Cache, where low water compelled us to again unload our goods in order to pass our boats over the shoal that here presented itself; and again we camped after a hard day's labor.

Isle La Cache took its name from a circumstance in the life of Mr. Sara, a trader who, when on his way with loaded canoes from Montreal to St. Louis, with goods for the Indian trade on the Ohio River, camped at this point. A band of Indians demanded of him some of his goods as a tribute for the privilege of passing down the river; this was refused. The Indians then returned to their village, a short distance below, held a council and determined to stop his canoes as he passed their village, and take by force what he had refused to give. Some of them, however, opposed this robbery, and one of the band reported the action of the council to Mr. Sara.

The night was dark and misty, and Mr. Sara determined to pass if possible by strategy, but to fight rather than accede to their demands. Fearing he might be overcome by numbers and thus lose his goods, and in order to lighten his canoes, so that he could pass rapidly over the shoal places in the river, he ordered the most valuable portion of his goods removed to a grove, about a mile distant on the prairie, and there hid them in holes dug in the ground (caches), removing the surplus earth to a distance, and carefully smoothing over the spot, so that no trace of the hiding place could be seen; he then armed his men with guns, tomahawks, and knives, and at daybreak started on his way down the river.

Stopping at the village, he stationed his men so as to guard the canoes, and then called on the Indians for a talk, which was granted; he told them that he should defend his goods; that the Great Father, the French King. had given him permission to go to the Ohio River, and showed them a parchment ornamented with numerous ribbons and large red seals; he said to them, '' here is my evidence, the King has made this writing, and it tells you that I must not be stopped or disturbed in passing through the nations of his red children; if any harm shall come to me he will revenge it by sending an army to destroy them and take possession of their country.''

This speech and demonstration had the desired effect, and the Indians were glad to excuse themselves; they however said that they were poor and needed clothing and tobacco; that they had no powder and but few guns, and were preparing to send a delegation to St. Louis to see their Great Father's Captain to state their condition and make known their wants.

Mr. Sara replied that he was authorized to give them a present from their Great Father, and that he should have done so but for their demand and threat, but as they had repented, he would now give it to them; whereupon he handed them a small bale, which he had previously prepared for that purpose, and ornamented with ribbons and sealing wax. The bale contained a few pieces of calico, powder and shot, tobacco and flints, and steels for striking fire, which delighted them exceedingly.

He then said to them, '' You see my canoes are light; I have but little in them, but when I camped last night you saw them heavily loaded. I had a dream; the Spirit told me you held a council, and determined to rob me when I passed your village this morning; that is why you see my men with guns, tomahawks, and knives, with which to defend themselves; we did not fear you, though there are many of you and we are but few, though you might have overpowered us; we are now friends, and I want you to help us; go with my men, take your pack-horses and bring the goods I have left behind and help us down the river with our boats until we reach the deep water below the shoals, when I will give you another bale of goods in token of my friendship, and bid you farewell." To this they consented; the goods were removed from their hiding place and transported on horses to the confluence of the Desplaines and Kankakee Rivers and again loaded in the canoes; the Indians being both surprised and amused at his strategy. This is the story as related to me.

Our progress from this point was very slow indeed, and most of the distance to the Illinois River our goods were carried on our backs, while our lightened boats were pulled over the shallow places, often being compelled to place poles under them, and on these drag them over the rocks and shoals. In this manner almost three weeks were occupied in reaching the mouth of Fox River, and two days more brought us to the foot of Starved Rock. Parkman, in his Discovery of the Great West, thus describes this romantic and picturesque spot :

" The cliff called 'Starved Rock,' now pointed out to travelers as the chief natural curiosity of the region, rises steep on three sides as a castle wall to the height of a hundred and twenty-five feet above the river. In front, it overhangs the water that washes its base; its western brow looks down on the tops of the forest trees below ; and on the east lies a wide gorge or ravine, choked with the mingled foliage of oaks, walnuts, and elms; while in its rocky depths a little brook creeps down to mingle with the river.

"From the rugged trunk of the stunted cedar that leans forward from the brink, you may drop a plummet into the river below, where the catfish and the turtles may plainly be seen gliding over the wrinkled sands of the clear shallow current. The cliff is accessible only from behind, where a man may climb up, not without difficulty, by a steep and narrow passage. The top is about an acre in extent." *

After leaving Starved Rock we met with no further detentions from scarcity of water. We passed on our way a number of Indian villages and stopped a few hours at each, not for the purpose of trading, but only to barter tobacco and powder for meat and Indian corn. We were treated kindly by all, and felt perfectly safe among them ; they were all acquainted with our traders, and knew where the trading houses were to be located, from which they would obtain their hunting outfits.

Opposite the mouth of Bureau River, and about a mile above the present site of the town of Hennepin, our first trading house was located, and placed in charge of Mr. Beebeau, who for many years had been a trader in that region. I was assigned to this post and was to have charge of the accounts, as neither Beebeau nor any of the men could read or write. Beebeau kept his accounts with the Indians by a system of hieroglyphics.

I was permitted by Mr. Deschamps to accompany him to St. Louis, whither he went with one boat to pur-

* The Discovery of the Great West, p. 287-8.

chase supplies of tobacco and some other needed articles from the French people at Cahokia. Beebeau received his invoices of goods and detail of men, and we proceeded onward.

Our next post was located three miles below Lake Peoria, and about sixty miles from Bureau, and was placed in charge of old Mr. Beason, a venerable man, who had long been a trader on this river, and was well and favorably known by the Indians : this we called Opa post.

As we rounded the point of the lake above Peoria, we discovered that old Fort Clark was on fire, and upon reaching it we found Indians to the number of about two hundred engaged in a war dance ; they were hideously painted, and had scalps on their spears and in their sashes, which they had taken from Americans during the war with Great Britain from 1812 to 1815.

A young brave having noticed me, inquired who I was, and Mr. Deschamps replied that I was his adopted son from Montreal. This answer he gave to allay the suspicion that had arisen that I was an American, a nation then much disliked by the Indians.

The Indian doubted the truth of Mr. Deschamps' statement, insisted that I was an American, and endeavored to force a quarrel with me. Mr. Dechamps left me in the boat in charge of one of the men, and went among the Indians to converse with them.

Using this man as an interpreter, the Indian resumed the conversation with me, and saying that I was an American, took from his sash, one after another, a number of scalps, and showing them to me, told me they were the scalps of my people. I was trembling with fear, which he observed, and drawing from his sash a long-haired scalp, he wet it and sprinkled the water in my face. In a moment my fear turned to rage, and seizing Mr. Deschamps' double-barreled gun, which lay in the bottom of the boat, I took deliberate aim at him and fired. The man who was left with me, seeing my intention, struck up the gun and saved the Indian's life, and probably my own and that of others of our party. Hearing the report of the gun and the consequent confusion, Mr. Deschamps and the men with him came running back to the boats, and after a short consultation Mr. Deschamps ordered the boats to push out, and we started down the stream. This incident left such an impression on my mind that no doubt exists with me as to the time of the burning of Fort Clark.

Having given Mr. Beason his outfit and left with him one of our boats, we pursued our journey, establishing posts every sixty miles, the last one being about fifty miles above the mouth of the river.

From this point we departed with but one boat, with a picked crew of men, all in high glee and singing a Canadian boat song, in which Mr. Deschamps, as usual, led. We made rapid progress, and when we again camped it was at the mouth of the Illinois River. On the following day, November sixth, at about two o'clock in the afternoon, we reached St. Louis. Our boat was soon surrounded by the friends of Mr. Deschamps, among whom were many priests, and all united in a hearty greeting.

I knew my father and brother should be at this place, but where to find them I could not tell. My anxiety to see them was so great that I went into the nearest tavern, but found no trace of them there. As I was on the street I passed a gentleman who seemed to notice me; I turned and spoke to him, telling him I was a stranger in search of my father. He thought a moment, then said, "The name sounds familiar; I think I was introduced to him at Mr. Paddock's." I asked him if Mr. Paddock came from Vermont; he replied in the affirmative, and directed me to his house, which I soon found. The door was opened by a pretty young girl,* who told me that he was at Mr. Enos', who was also a Vermonter and an old friend of our family. Here at last I found my father, who was conversing with Mr. Enos. He did not recognize me, so much had I changed since our parting, though only six months had passed. I was then thin and pale from close confinement in the store, but with the outdoor life and exposure. I had gained in weight and strength, and become as brown as an Indian.

On inquiring for my brother, I learned that he was employed in a drug store near by, where we found him pounding something in a mortar. Though I did not speak he knew me at once, and exclaimed, "O, brother! brother!" bursting into tears. The meeting was a joyous one, and I think the day the happiest of my life.

At this time St. Louis had a population of about eight hundred, composed of French, English, Spanish, and American.

Cahokia, a French town on the opposite side of the river, was then the largest, it having a population of

---

*About two years previous to the death of Mr. Hubbard, Miss Paddock, the "pretty young girl," of 1818, was reminded of this incident by reading a published letter of Mr. Hubbard's, and immediately wrote him, giving her address, after which several letters passed between them.

about one thousand. There Mr. Deschamps made most of his purchases of flour and tobacco, which, with some merchandise bought in St. Louis, completed our return cargo.

This French village was then a jolly place. Mr. Deschamps was a favorite with all, and was treated as the distinguished guest of every family. There was dancing at some of the houses every night; and even the priests claimed his assistance in their singing.

I was permitted to remain in St. Louis with my father and brother, being required to report daily to Mr. Deschamps, and perform such duties as were assigned to me. My home was at Mr. Paddock's, with my brother, and here I was treated very kindly by all the family. My father was preparing to go to Arkansas, with the intention of locating permanently there; and when, at the end of two weeks, we parted, it was our farewell, as I never saw him again.

About the twentieth of November we started on our
return voyage, ascending the Mississippi and Illinois Rivers and distributing to our various trading posts portions
of our cargo. I reached my station between the tenth
and fifteenth of December, where Mr. Deschamps, after giving me particular instructions as to my duties, and opening the books, left me with his blessing. The accounts had
heretofore been kept in hieroglyphics by Beebeau, my
ignorant master, who proved to be sickly, cross, and petu-
lant. He spent the greater part of his time in bed,
attended by a fat, dirty Indian woman, a doctress, who
made and administered various decoctions to him. One
of our men, Antoine, had an Indian wife and two
children, the oldest a boy about my own age, but who
was not regularly in the employ of the Company.

My trouble at Fort Clark, and the circumstances at-
tending it, had become known to the Indians in the vicinity of our post. Their chief was Wa-ba, and soon after
my arrival he, accompanied by Shaub-e-nee, called on
me, saying they wished to see the little American brave.
Shaub-e-nee was then about twenty-five years of age,

4 (49)

and was, I thought, the finest looking man I had ever seen. He was fully six feet in height, finely proportioned, and with a countenance expressive of intelligence, firmness and kindness. He was one of Tecumseh's aids at the battle of the Thames, being at his side when Tecumseh was shot. Becoming disgusted with the conduct of General Proctor, he, with Billy Caldwell (the Sauganash), withdrew their support from the British and espoused the cause of the Americans. Shaub-e-nee, in after years, during the Black Hawk War, was indefatigable in notifying the white settlers in DuPage, Grundy, and La Salle Counties of threatened danger, often riding both night and day, in great peril, and by his timely warning and counsel saving the lives of many settlers. He lived to the age of eighty-four years, and died July 17, 1859, at his home in Morris, Grundy County, respected and beloved by all who knew him.

Chief Wa-ba had shortly before this lost a son, of about my own age, and so, according to the Indian custom, he adopted me in his stead, naming me Che-mo-co-mon-ess (the Little American). I enjoyed the friendship of Wa-ba for a number of years and until his death, and I here desire to deny the statement made by a historian of our State, that Wa-ba plundered certain mounds and removed from them their valuable contents. Such a deed would have been wholly at variance with his character, which was that of an honest man, and certainly could not have occured without my having heard of it, which I never did until I saw it in the book referred to.

Wa-ba had another son who, with Antoine's son and myself, frequently hunted together, and we all became quite expert.

Our cabin was built of logs, those forming the sides being laid one on the other and held in place by stakes driven into the ground, and these fastened together at the top by withes of bark. The logs forming the ends were of smaller size, driven into the ground perpendicularly, the centre ones being longer and forked at the top, and upon these rested the ridge pole. Straight-grained logs were then selected and split as thin as possible, making sections of three or four inches in thickness, which were laid with one end resting upon the ridge pole, the other on the logs which formed the sides of the cabin; through these was driven a wooden pin, which rested against the top log on the inside of the cabin, and projected eighteen inches or two feet above the roof. The cracks and openings of roof and sides were then daubed with a cement made of clay mixed with ashes, and then the whole roof was covered with long grass, which was held in place by other logs laid on top.

The chimney and fire place were made in the following manner: At the centre of one side of the room four straight poles were driven firmly in the ground, the front ones being about eight feet apart and the back ones about five feet; then small saplings, cut to proper lengths, were fastened by withes at each end to the upright poles, and about eighteen inches apart. Then came the mortar, made from clay and ashes, into which was kneaded long grass so as to form strips ten or twelve inches in width and about four feet long; the centre of these strips were then placed or hung on the cross poles and pressed together so as to cover the wood, and in this way the chimney was carried up to the top of the upright poles and then three or four feet above the roof, or even with the ridge pole. A second coat of mortar, about two-inches thick, was then thrown on, pressed to the rough first coat and smoothed with the hands; the hearth was then made of dry, stiff clay, pounded down hard, and the structure was finished.

The floor of the cabin was made of puncheons, the surface of which were dressed with a common axe or tomahawk, so as to remove the splinters, the edges being made to fit together as close as possible. The door was made of the same material, puncheons, hung on wooden hinges, and fastened by a wooden latch with back string attached, so it could be raised from the outside, and when the string was pulled in, the door was locked.

To make the window one of the logs in the end of the cabin was cut so as to leave an opening of about eighteen inches in width by twenty or thirty inches in length, into which was set a rough sash, and over this was pasted or glued paper, which had been thoroughly oiled with bear or coon grease. This completed the house, which was warm and comfortable.

Our bunks were placed in a row, one above the other, and were made of puncheons split as thin as possible. The bottom rested on parallel saplings cut to a proper length, one end of which was inserted in a two-inch auger hole in the logs of the cabin, and the other supported by a puncheon set upright. The bedding consisted of long, coarse grass, laid lengthwise of the bunk, on top of which was placed a skin of some kind (generally buckskin) or an Indian mat. At the head the grass was raised so as to make a pillow, and to each man was allowed one blanket for cover.

The table, with round sapling legs, and puncheon top, and a three-legged stool, constructed in the same manner, completed the furniture of the mansion.

The only tools allowed to each outfit was a common axe, a two-inch auger, an ordinary scalping knife, a crooked knife (this had a blade six inches long and rounded at the end), and tomahawk, and with these implements everything was constructed, and some of the men did excellent work with these simple tools.

Our kitchen utensels were few and primitive, consisting of a frying-pan, a couple of tin pots, one very large Indian bowl made of wood, and several smaller ones. Table knives and forks we had none, and our spoons were of wood, ranging in capacity from a gill to a pint.

Wood was, of course, plenty, and our large fire-place was kept well filled.

A camp-kettle chain was suspended from a hook made from the limb of a tree and fastened to the roof, from which also hung cords, which were used for roasting game. Our meat being thus suspended before a bright fire, it was the duty of one man, with a long stick, to keep it whirling rapidly until sufficiently cooked, when it was placed in the large wooden bowl on the table, and each one helped himself by cutting off with his knife and fingers as much as he desired. Usually we had nothing else on the table except honey. The wild turkey was used as a substitute for bread, and when eaten with fat venison, coon, or bear, is more delicious than any roast can be.

One of our luxuries, which was reserved for special occasions, was corn soup, and this was always acceptable.

Those traders who were so fortunate as to possess an

iron bake-pan or skillet, were particularly favored, and the more so if they were also possessed of flour, for then many delicacies were possible, and many kinds of chopped meats and baked " avingnols " afforded a dish not to be refused by kings.

Let me give one or two recipes : To one pound of lean venison, add one pound of the breast of turkey, three-fourths of a pound of the fat of bear or raccoon ; salt and pepper to taste, and season with the wild onion or leek; chop up or pound fine (the meat), and mix all well together ; then make a thin crust, with which cover the sides and bottom of the bake-pan ; then put in the meat and cover it with a thicker crust, which must be attached firmly to the side crust ; now put on the cover of your bake-pan and set it on the hot coals, heaping them on the top, and bake for one hour, and you will have a delicious dish.

Another : Make a thin batter and drop small balls of the minced meat into it and fry in bear or coon fat, taking care that the meat is well covered with the batter. This we called " les avingnol."

From the ponds we gathered the seeds of the lotus, which we used for coffee, our ever-filled honey-trough furnishing the sweetening. Our supply of salt and pepper was rather limited, and these were used only on special occasions.

Thus passed the winter. When at home, chatting, joking and playing tricks on each other; making oars and paddles to replace the worn out and broken ones, and getting ourselves ready for the spring's departure.

As I had little to do in the house besides keeping the books and being present when sales were made for furs or on credit, and being disgusted with the disagreeable and filthy habits of my master, Beebeau, I fairly lived in the open air with my two comrades. Our time was spent in the manly exercise of hunting and trapping, on foot or in canoes, and as they spoke in the Indian language only, they were of great assistance to me in learning it, which I accomplished before spring. I also became proficient in hunting, and could discern animal tracks on the ground and tell what kind they were, and whether they were walking slow or fast or running. I could detect the marks on the trunks of trees made by such animals as the raccoon or panther, if they had made it a retreat within a month or so. My companions had many laughs and jokes at my expense for my awkwardness in hunting and ignorance in tracking animals, but I faithfully persevered in my education.

My clothing during this winter and for the subsequent years of my life as a trader, consisted of a buckskin hunting shirt or a blue capote belted in at the waist with a sash or buckskin belt, in which was carried a knife and sheath, a tomahawk, and a tobacco pouch made of the skin of some animal, usually otter or mink. In the pouch was carried a flint and steel and piece of punk.

Underneath my outside garment I wore a calico shirt, breech-cloth, and buckskin leggins. On my feet *neips and moccasins, and sometimes in winter, a red knit cap on my head. I allowed my hair to grow long and usually went bareheaded. When traveling in winter I carried, and sometimes wore, a blanket.

During this winter I made two trips into the interior:

---

* Square pieces of blanket which were folded over the feet, and were worn in place of stockings.

One to the mouth of Rock River, where I first saw Black Hawk, and for the first time slept in an Indian wigwam. The other to the Wabash River. For the privilege of going, I was required to carry a pack on my back of fifty pounds weight, the men with me carrying eighty pounds. These packs contained goods to exchange for furs and peltries. During the first few days this was very severe, and I often wished I had not undertaken it, but by the time I returned. I was able to carry my pack with comparative ease and keep up with the others in walking.

On my trip to the Wabash River we found a band of Kick-a-poo Indians encamped on Pine Creek, a branch of the Wabash, and one evening quite a number of the Indians gathered into the trader's wigwam and were discussing the subject of Harrison's fight at Tippecanoe. A number of these Indians had participated in the battle, and twelve of them had been wounded. As I could not understand their language sufficiently well to converse, I employed my man as interpreter, and told them that from what I had read in books, they had deceived General Harrison, pretending to be friendly and getting him to camp in an exposed situation where an attacking enemy would have great advantages. They laughed heartily, saying that the contrary was the truth. He had selected the strongest natural position in all that country; that at any other place they could have conquered him and but few could have escaped. In consequence of his strong position, they had a long consultation in planning the attack. I was so much interested in what I heard that I asked to go to the battle ground on the following morning, which they agreed to. Accordingly, the next morning I was furnished with a pony, and accompanied by two or three of them, started for the battle ground, and on arriving there found that their report was correct, and was much surprised at seeing such a location.

The ground was admirably adapted to defense, being on an elevated plateau. On the westerly side ran Burnett Creek, the bank of which, on the side of Harrison's encampment, was very steep, while on the opposite side the descent was gradual. On the easterly side was a prairie swamp skirting the plateau. Northerly and easterly was high ground and timber land, and it was here and along the creek that Harrison's soldiers made the attack. From Harrison's Report, pp. 289-290, it appears that General Harrison did not quite like the ground, but I am satisfied that no better could have been found in that vicinity, and in that opinion I am sustained by General Tipton, who participated in the battle, and with whom I afterwards became acquainted while he was Indian agent at Logansport, Ind.

At a subsequent date I again visited the locality in company with General Tipton, and he pointed out to me the positions held by the contending forces, and his account of the battle agreed with that given me by my red friends. The general and myself seated ourselves under a tree, on the bank of the little creek where the Kick-a-poos made their attack, and he there detailed to me the incidents of the march and fight. With a small stick he mapped out on the ground the positions held by the troops and Indians, and, playfully digging and throwing up pebbles, he said: "Near this spot a friend of mine had his jaw shot away; he suffered great agony, but soon died." Just as he said this he unearthed some teeth which had once belonged to a human being. He picked them up, firmly believing them to be those of his friend, and for years after they occupied a place in his cabinet of curiosities.

Our trip proved a successful one, and having sold all our goods, we hired ponies to transport our furs and peltries and returned home, where I was warmly welcomed by my young companions, who were glad to have me again join them in their hunts. A day sufficed to decipher Beebeau's hieroglyphics, extract from memorandas and memory, the items of accounts, and write up the books, and I dropped back into the regular routine of my life. I also made a visit to our trading post situated three miles below Peoria, which was in charge of old Mr. Beason. Though this post was sixty miles distant we reached it in one day's travel by starting at daylight and walking until dark, and returned after a visit of two or three days. By constant practice I had by this time become a good walker and could cover forty to fifty miles per day with ease.

Winter passed without any special incident, and early in March, 1819, we received by a carrier orders from Mr. Deschamps to have every thing in complete readiness to start for Mackinaw on the twentieth. We kept track of the days of the month by notches cut in a stick, which hung in the store, having no almanac or calendar, and indeed I was the only one of the party who could have read it if we had possessed one.

Our fare had consisted during the winter of a variety of game, such as venison, raccoon, panther, bear, and turkey, varied as spring approached with swan, geese and crane, besides almost every variety of duck. Prairie chickens and quail were also abundant, but these we did not consider eatable. Our game was cooked in French style, and to our mind, could not be excelled in any kitchen.

We had received in the fall one pound of green tea and a bag of flour, about a hundred pounds, and while this lasted we luxuriated on Sundays in pancakes and honey. The woods abounded in wild honey, and we kept a large wooden bowl full at all times, of which we partook whenever we desired.

In the forenoon of the 20th of March, we heard in the distance the sound of the familiar boat-song and recognized the rich tones of Mr. Deschamps' voice, and we knew the "Brigade" was coming. We all ran to the landing and soon saw Mr. Deschamps' boat rounding the point about a mile below; his ensign floating in the breeze. We shouted with joy at their arrival and gave them a hearty welcome.

The remainder of the day and far into the night was spent in exchanging friendly greetings and recounting the events that had transpired since our parting. Little sleep was had, and but little wanted. Mr. Deschamps had flour and tobacco, and we feasted and smoked and talked and laughed, and a happier party cannot well be imagined. The next day we spent in loading our boats, and the day following the thirteen boats of the "Brigade" pushed off from the shore, and, to the music of the Canadian boat-song, we started on our long return journey.

The first night we halted at our old camp-ground at the foot of Starved Rock. From this point until we reached Cache Island, our progress was very slow, averag-

ing but from six to ten miles per day. The river was
high, the current swift, and the rapids strong, and as
the boats were heavily laden and a cold storm prevailed,
we were glad to camp early and afford the men a much-
needed rest. Early the morning following we left Cache
Island, and as the wind was strong from the southwest,
we hoisted our square sails for the first time, and rapidly
passed up the Desplaines River, through Mud Lake, to
South Branch, regardless of the course of the channel,
and soon reached Chicago.

We camped on the north side of the river, a small distance above Fort Dearborn, where we remained six or
eight days repairing our boats and putting them in condition for the more serious journey of coasting Lake
Michigan.

Our stay in Chicago was a pleasant one to me. The
same officers were in command at the fort that were
there when we left in the fall, and warmly greeted us
on our return.

Mr. Kinzie again took me to his own house, where I
was treated as one of the family, and I formed a strong
attachment for these good friends. Seeing Mrs. Kinzie
again brought my mother vividly to my mind, and made
me all the more anxious to hear from her and my father.
Since parting from them I had not heard from either,
and could not expect to until I reached Mackinaw.

On a beautiful morning in April, about the 20th or
25th, we left Chicago and camped at the Grand Calumet.
We did not desire to reach the mouth of Grand River
(Grand Haven) before the May full moon, for annually
at that time the Indians assembled to fast and feast their
dead, the ceremonies occupying eight or ten days. A

noted burying ground was selected and the ground around the graves thoroughly cleaned, they being put in the best of order. Many of the graves were marked by small poles, to which were attached pieces of white cloth. These preparations having been completed, all except the young children blackened their faces with charcoal and fasted for two whole days, eating literally nothing during that time. Though many of them had no relatives buried there, all joined in the fast and ceremonies in memory of their dead who were buried elsewhere, and the sounds of mourning and lamentation were heard around the graves and in the wigwams.

At the close of the two days' fast they washed their faces, put on their decorations, and commenced feasting and visiting from one wigwam to another. They now placed wooden dishes at the head of each grave, which were kept daily supplied with food, and were protected from the dogs, wolves, and other animals, by sticks driven into the ground around and inclosing them. The feasting lasted several days, and the ceremonies were concluded by their celebrated game of ball, which is intensely interesting, even the dogs becoming excited and adding to the commotion by mixing with the players and barking and racing around the grounds.

We progressed leisurely to the mouth of the St. Joseph River, where we encamped for several days, and were joined by the traders from that river. We reached Grand River early in May, and sought a good camping place up the river, some distance from the Indian camps. The "Feast of the Dead" had commenced, and many Indians had already arrived, and for five or six days we were witnesses to their strange yet solemn ceremonies.

One evening, at the close of the feast, we were informed that an Indian, who the fall previous, in a drunken quarrel, had killed one of the sons of a chief of the Manistee band, would on the morrow deliver himself up to suffer the penalty of his crime according to the Indian custom. We gave but little credence to the rumor, though the Indians seemed much excited over it. On the following day, however, the rumor proved true, and I witnessed the grandest and most thrilling incident of my life.

The murderer was a Canadian Indian, and had no blood relatives among the Manistees, but had by invitation, returned with some of the tribe from Malden, where they received their annuities from the English Government, and falling in love with a Manistee maiden, had married her and settled among them, agreeing to become one of their tribe. As was customary, all his earnings from hunting and trapping belonged to his father-in-law until the birth of his first child, after which he commanded his time and could use his gains for the benefit of his family. At the time of the killing of the chief's son he had several children and was very poor, possessing nothing but his meagre wearing apparel and a few traps. He was a fair hunter, but more proficient as a trapper.

Knowing that his life would be taken unless he could ransom it with furs and articles of value, after consulting with his wife, he determined to depart at night in a canoe with his family and secretly make his way to the marshes at the headwaters of the Muskegon River, where he had before trapped successfully, and there endeavor to catch beaver, mink, marten, and other fine furs,

which were usually abundant, and return in the spring
and satisfy the demands of the chief.   As, according to
the custom, if he failed to satisfy the chief and family of
the murdered man, either by ransom or a sacrifice of his
own life, they could demand of his wife's brothers what
he had failed to give, he consulted with one of them
and told him of his purpose, and designated a particular
location on the Muskegon where he could be found if it
became necessary for him to return and deliver himself
up.   Having completed his arrangements, he made his
escape and arrived safely at the place of destination, and
having but few traps and but a small supply of ammunition, he arranged dead-fall traps in a circuit around
his camp, hoping with them and his few traps to have a
successful winter, and by spring to secure enough to save
his life.

After the burial of his son, the chief took counsel with
his sons as to what they should do to revenge the dead,
and as they knew the murderer was too poor to pay their
demands, they determined upon his death, and set about
finding him.   Being disappointed in this, they made a
demand upon the brothers of his wife, who, knowing
that they could not satisfy his claims, counselled together
as to what course to pursue, all but one of them believing he had fled to Canada.

The younger brother, knowing his whereabouts, sent
word to the chief that he would go in search of the murderer, and if he failed to produce him would himself give
his own life in his stead.   This being acceptable, without
divulging the secret of his brother-in-law's hiding place,
he started to find him.   It was a long and difficult journey, as he had no landmarks to go by and only knew

that he should find his brother-in-law on the headwaters of the Muskegon, which he finally did.

The winter had been one of unusually deep snow, and the spring one of great floods, which had inundated the country where he was. The bears had kept in their dens, and for some reason the marten, beavers, and mink had not been found, so that when their brother-in-law reached them he and his family were almost perishing from starvation, and his winter's hunt had proved unsuccessful. They accordingly descended together to the main river, where the brother left them for his return home, it being agreed between them that the murderer would himself report at the mouth of Grand River during the "Feast of the Dead," which promise he faithfully performed.

Soon after sunrise the news spread through the camp that he was coming. The chief hastily selected a spot in a valley between the sand-hills, in which he placed himself and family in readines to receive him, while we traders, together with the Indians, sought the surrounding sand-hills, that we might have a good opportunity to witness all that should occur. Presently we heard the monotonous thump of the Indian drum, and soon thereafter the mournful voice of the Indian, chanting his own death song, and then we beheld him, marching with his wife and children, slowly and in single file, to the place selected for his execution, still singing and beating the drum.

When he reached a spot near where sat the chief, he placed the drum on the ground, and his wife and children seated themselves on mats which had been prepared for them. He then addressed the chief, saying: "I, in a drunken moment, stabbed your son, being provoked to it by his accusing me of being a coward and calling me an old woman. I fled to the marshes at the head of the Muskegon, hoping that the Great Spirit would favor me in the hunt, so that I could pay you for your lost son. I was not successful. Here is the knife with which I killed your son; by it I wish to die. Save my wife and children. I am done." The chief received the knife, and, handing it to his oldest son, said, "Kill him." The son advanced, and, placing his left hand upon the shoulder of his victim, made two or three feints with the knife and then plunged it into his breast to the handle and immediately withdrew it.

Not a murmur was heard from the Indian or his wife and children. Not a word was spoken by those assembled to witness. All nature was silent, broken only by the singing of the birds. Every eye was turned upon the victim, who stood motionless with his eyes firmly fixed upon his executioner, and calmly received the blow without the appearance of the slightest tremor. For a few moments he stood erect, the blood gushing from the wound at every pulsation; then his knees began to quake; his eyes and face assumed an expression of death, and he sank upon the sand.

During all this time the wife and children sat perfectly motionless, gazing upon the husband and father. Not a sigh or a murmur escaping their lips until life was extinct, when they threw themselves upon his dead body, lying in a pool of blood, in grief and lamentations, bringing tears to the eyes of the traders, and causing a murmur of sympathy to run through the multitude of Indians.

Turning to Mr. Deschamps, down whose cheeks the

tears were trickling. I said : "Why did you not save that noble Indian. A few blankets and shirts, and a little cloth, would have done it." "Oh, my boy," he replied, "we should have done it. It was wrong and thoughtless in us. What a scene we have witnessed."

Still the widowed wife and her children were clinging to the dead body in useless tears and grief. The chief and his family sat motionless for fifteen or twenty minutes, evidently regretting what had been done. Then he arose, approached the body, and in a trembling voice said : "Woman stop weeping. Your husband was a brave man, and like a brave, was not afraid to die as the rules of our nation demanded. We adopt you and your children in the place of my son ; our lodges are open to you ; live with any of us ; we will treat you like our own sons and daughters ; you shall have our protection and love." "Che-qui ock" (that is right), was heard from the assembled Indians, and the tragedy was ended.

That scene is indelibly stamped on my mind, never to be forgotten.

After the conclusion of the feast, we left in company with a large fleet of birch-bark canoes, occupied by Indians and their families, returning from their winter hunting grounds to their villages on the shore of Lake Michigan. A fair wind at starting increased to a gale in the after part of the day, and caused a high sea. We reached the Manistee River, which had a strong current, in entering which, we experienced much trouble from the breakers, and some of the boats shipped considerable water, but we all landed in safety. The Indians, however, were not so fortunate, some of their canoes being swamped, and several of the women and children drowned. No assistance could be rendered them, though a number of the children, who were lashed to bundles of Indian mats, were saved; the Indians and squaws swimming and holding to the mats, and thus keeping them from turning over. Others were saved by the canoes that followed, and passed safely in

We reached Mackinaw without further incident about the middle of May, being among the first to arrive from the Indian country. Other "outfits" followed shortly after, the last to arrive being from the Lake of the Woods.

I found letters from my mother awaiting me, one of which announced the death of my father, which occurred soon after he reached Arkansas. He was taken sick while on the circuit. Having been but a short time in the Territory, he had formed but few acquaintances, and those mostly lawyers. My little brother, Christopher, thus suddenly left, was kindly cared for by R. P. Spalding, Esq., an attorney of the Territory, whose father resided in Norwich, Conn., and in the following winter his kind protector took him to Middletown, Conn., where he found friends and relatives.

My mother had left Montreal and returned to New England, and had with her, her youngest daughter, Hannah, while my other sisters had been placed at school, one in Windsor, Vt., and the others in New London, Conn.; thus were those most dear to me, and to each other, cast upon the world without home or protector. This news made me very sad, and I determined to return and care for my mother and family, and accordingly tendered my resignation, which the Company refused to accept.

After a few days' sojourn I was detailed under Mr. Matthews to receive and help count the furs brought in by the different oufits, put them into packs, and get them in readiness for shipment to New York, whither they were to go in a vessel chartered at Buffalo for that purpose. This packing furs was very hard work, and about one hundred men were detailed to assist in it. Each skin must be beaten to remove the dust and any moths that might be in it. The different qualities were then carefully selected, and each packed into a frame, which was put under a press made of strong upright planks, on each side of which were four-inch openings, and in these were placed oak scantling, which filled the space between the top of the pack and the head of the frame. Wedges were then introduced between the scantling and these driven in by wooden mauls, as heavy as one man could wield, until the furs would compress no further, when the pack was firmly tied at ends and centre with rawhide ropes. A stave was attached to each pack, under the ropes, upon which was marked the number. The number, quality and kind of skins were then correctly invoiced. Work commenced at five o'clock in the morning and lasted until sunset, with an intermission of one hour at noon. My duties did not, however, end with sunset. I had to lock up before I went to my supper, and after to write up the accounts of the day, which often took until midnight. This was the commencement for me of real hard work, and lasted five or six weeks.

Robert Stewart had charge of the outside work, while Mr. Crooks was the general director of the affairs of the Company. These two gentlemen were wholly unlike in character. Mr. Crooks was a mild man, rarely out of temper, and governed more by quiet reasoning and mild command than by dictation. Mr. Stewart was one of those stern Scotchmen, who gave his orders abruptly and expected them obeyed to the letter, yet a man of a deal of humor and fond of fun. He had a fund of anecdotes and was excellent company. Though he often gave unnecessary orders and required everything to be done neatly and promptly, he was kind and sympathetic. He was quick tempered and wholly fearless, and the clerks knew that his commands were to be obeyed to the letter, but that if their duties were properly performed they would receive full credit and be treated with kindness and consideration.

At one time, when he had sent men to Bois Blanc Island to cut the year's supply of wood, he learned that some of them had returned, and suspected that they had been sent for whisky. He accordingly caused them to be watched until his suspicions were confirmed. When they were about to push off for their return he suddenly appeared, expressing great surprise to see them. "What is the matter," said he; "have you met with an accident; are any of you sick, or what are you here for?" The bowman replied that they came over to see some friends and get tobacco, and proceeded to push the boat off. Mr. Stewart rushed into the water and seized the boat by its bow; two of the men persisted in pushing it off, but he succeeded in pulling the boat ashore, and ordered the two men up into the yard. Closing the gate, he told them they were to be punished, and they, being very angry, used insulting language, which threw him into a towering rage. Seizing a stick he knocked them both down, nearly killing one of them. Dr. Beaumont, the surgeon of the fort, was sent for, who examined the man, and pronounced his skull fractured and the result doubtful. Mr. Stewart was in great distress and himself cared for the man through the night, and was much relieved in his mind when the doctor told him in the morning that he thought the man would live, though a slight increase in the force of the blow would certainly have killed him.

This Mr. Stewart was the same man described by Mr. Irving in his "Astoria," as having compelled the captain of the ship in which he was sailing to tack ship and return to an island for his uncle, who had gone ashore while the vessel was becalmed and had accidentally been left there.

My good friend, John H. Kinzie, resided in Mr. Stewart's family, and though much loved and respected, was often the victim of his temper or humor. On one occasion, when he had finished making out a long invoice, which he had taken unusual care to write nicely and in commercial shape, and supposed he would be highly complimented on its production, delivered it to Mr. Stewart, who carefully looked it over, sheet after sheet, and on the very last page discovered a blot and a figure erased and rewritten. Pointing to them with a scowl, he said, "Do you call this well done ? Go and do it over"; and he tore it into fragments. Poor John was sorely mortified, but was consoled by Mrs. Stewart, who had been instructed to do so by her husband, and proceeded to rewrite his invoice, satisfied either of his own imperfections, or of the disagreeable temper of his master.

At another time, an old *voyageur* who performed the

duties of a house-servant for Mr. Stewart, complained to him that John was impertinent to him, ordering him to do things instead of politely asking him to, and said that at times he was tempted to strike him. "You are right, old man," said Mr. Stewart. "The boy is foolish; he should always treat an old man with respect; give him a good thrashing the next time he insults you; if you do not I shall have to. Can you whip him in a fair fight?" "Yes, sir," was the reply. "Then do so; but be sure you strike him with nothing but your fist." When John came to dinner he told him to order the old man to shovel the snow from a little yard in front of Mrs. Stewart's window. "Make him do it at once, and stand over him until it is done." The old man was busy sawing wood in a shed when John started to give him orders. As soon as John was out of the way, Mr. Stewart slipped into another room to a window to see the fun. John approached the old man, saying, "Old man, you have wood enough sawed; get the snow-shovel and clean away the snow from the little yard." The old man made no reply, but placed his thumb to his nose and made an expressive movement with his fingers. "Did you hear me?" "Yes." "Why don't you mind?" "None of your business; you wait till I get ready." "Ready or not, you have got to clean away the snow right off." "Who will make me?" "I," said John, and, advancing, rather unceremoniously put his hand on the old man's shoulder, who resented by a blow on the nose that started the blood. They fought for some time, to the great enjoyment of Mr. Stewart, and the lesson was not wholly lost either on John or the other clerks.

One evening when a number of clerks were sitting on

the stoop just after tea, Jean Baptiste Beaubien came along boasting of his fast running. Mr. Stewart had slipped up behind us unperceived and heard Beaubien's boasting, and said I can beat you in a race from the store to the cooper shop (about the distance of a block). "No, you can't," said Beaubien. "I will bet you a boot I can," said Stewart. "Done; come on," said Beaubien. So they took their stations and started. Mr. Stewart stopped about half-way, with Beaubien about a rod ahead; and, coming to the platform, said, "I'll pay the boot; but what will you do with only one boot?" Beaubien insisted that he was to have a pair, but on referring the matter to the parties, they decided the bet was for one only. "Now," said Mr. Stewart, "we will flip up a dollar to see whether it shall be a pair or none. Here is a dollar. Now, sir; heads I win, tails you lose. Three flips?" "Yes." It was head. "Oh, heads I win." Next time it turns tails. "Oh, tails you lose." "Yes, yes," says Beaubien. Throws again, and this time heads. "Heads I win, Mr. Beaubien." "How the d—l; 1 lose the head, I lose the tail; by gar, you make me lose all the time"; and, amid a roar of laughter, Mr. Stewart made his exit.

This Beaubien had some education, could read and write, and was very proud of his accomplishments. Coming into the office one morning about daylight he said to the bookkeeper, "Mr. Bookkeeper, I write very fine, and I make pretty figures." "Is that so? Well, help me a little; put down on that paper, one; now put down two; there, that's all; now add them together." After some reflection he announced the result as three. "Now," said the bookkeeper, "put down two; now one; add them together." After pondering over it for a time Beaubien looked up with a radiant countenance and exclaimed, " By gar he all make three," and went off profoundly impressed with his own learning and proficiency in mathematics.

I supposed I should be again detailed to the Illinois
river "brigade" with my old leader, Mr. Deschamps,
and was much surprised and grieved, when the time
arrived to select goods and make ready for our departure,
to receive one evening a summons from Mr. Crooks to
meet him at his private office, when I was informed that
I was not to go to my old post, but, in company with a
Frenchman named Jacques Dufrain, take charge of an
outfit on the Muskegon River. Dufrain could neither
read nor write, but had a large experience among the
Indians on the Peninsula of Michigan, and I was to be
governed by his advice in trading.

I was told that the invoices would be directed to me,
and that I was to be the commander of the expedition,
and Dufrain simply my adviser, and then I was not to
allow his advice to govern me when it differed materially
with my own views. Mr. Crooks also told me that
though I was young and inexperienced, he was confident
that with Dufrain's honesty and acquaintance with the
Indians, I would have no difficulty in conducting the
venture; the outfit would be small, and we were to go in

(74)

Mr. Deschamps' "brigade" to the mouth of the Muskegon or not, as we chose. Our headquarters were to be
some sixty miles up the river.

This was, indeed, a bitter disappointment to me, as I
had counted very much on seeing Mr. Kinzie's family,
for whom I had formed a great attachment, and had
hoped for Mr. Deschamps' permission to spend two or
three weeks with them and the officers of Fort Dearborn,
and then go alone and join my companions at Beaureau
trading house. And besides, I had left some of my clothing
at Mr. Kinzie's to be repaired and put in order by my
return. But as there was no other alternative, I received
my goods with a good grace, and about the middle of
October, 1819, started with the Illinois "brigade" on my
second trip to the Indian country.

We camped the first night at Point Wagashvic and
there remained wind-bound for the space of a week, and
soon thereafter reached the Little Traverse. Here Mr.
Deschamps advised me to stop and purchase my canoe
and some Indian corn. About ten miles distant, at the
foot of the bay, was an Indian village, and thither I
sent my associate to make the necessary purchases; and
after an absence of two days he returned with a canoe
loaded with Indians, and about eight bushels of corn and
some beans for our winter's stores. It was a small supply,
but all we could get, and having paid for it we got
ready to leave on the following morning.

When morning came we found the wind blowing
strong from the northeast, afterwards changing to northwest and west, and for ten days blowing a gale so that
November had come before we had started. We left
before the heavy sea had subsided, and with great labor

(there being but three men to row the boat) reached Grand Traverse, where we were again detained five or six days by adverse winds; another start, more heavy sea, and Calp River was reached, where we were again wind-bound for several days.

Thus, with a heavily laden canoe and adverse winds, often in great peril, sometimes shipping water and narrowly escaping wreck, suffering from cold, and worn with toil, we entered the Muskegon River about the tenth of December and found the lake frozen. The weather was very cold, and the coast Indians had all left for their hunting grounds in the interior.

Dufrain said it would be impossible to reach our destination, and recommended the repairing of an old abandoned trading house at a point of the lake about one and one half miles distant and there make our winter quarters. This we decided to do, though it would be very inconvenient, being from thirty to fifty miles distant from the Indian hunting grounds, where we should be compelled to go to trade. By breaking ice ahead of our boat we reached the place, and went industriously to work to repair the house and make it tenantable.

We had not seen an Indian for fifteen or twenty days, and as it was necessary to reach them, and let them know where we had located, we decided to send an expedition in search of them at once. Accordingly we made up an assortment of goods into three packages of about sixty pounds each, which, with a blanket apiece, were to be carried by Jacques and the two voyagers who constituted our force; and on a bright December morning they bade me good-bye and started on their journey.

As Jacques was perfectly familiar with the country,

I did not look forward to a long absence, and was content to remain alone. My stock of provisions consisted of the corn and a small quantity of flour, which we had brought from Mackinaw, and as I had my gun to depend on I thought I should have no difficulty in procuring all the meat I desired.

Dufrain had told me that I should find no game, but this I did not believe. I confined my hunting trips to a mile or so of the house, never daring to go out of sight of it, and for a week found rabbits and squirrels in sufficient numbers to supply me with food. Then came a heavy fall of snow and for several days I could find nothing to shoot, and as the work of walking in two feet of snow was very laborious and I expected Dufrain to return very soon, I concluded to remain in doors, keep up a good fire, and content myself with corn. I had, I think, three books, which helped me to while away the time.

We had found in the lake a drowned deer which we had skinned, and this skin dried furnished me with a mat upon which to lie in front of the fire. The fireplace was broad, some three or four feet, and very deep, and so took in large logs that made a warm, cheerful fire. The timber under the hill, around the house, had all been cut off by its former occupants, and procuring wood was a serious problem. Through the deep snow from the top of the hill I was obliged to carry it, and for days I labored all the morning in getting my day's supply of fuel. The snow being so deep I could not haul or roll it down the hill, I set about devising some way to overcome the difficulty, and the idea of using the deer skin in some way for a sled presented itself to my mind. As it was not long enough to take on the four-foot logs I cut them three feet only, and having soaked the skin to make it pliable, I laid a log on it, and tied up the sides of the skin around it with a grape vine, and found I had a pretty fair sled. My down-hill path soon became hard and smooth, and extended to the door of the house, and my load would frequently slide down to the bottom with me astride of it.

In a Book of Travels in the Northwest, which I had read, the author described the manner in which some tribes of Indians caught large fish during the winter. A hole was cut in the ice, over which a small shelter was built sufficiently large for one person to sit in, and made as dark as possible. The occupant then stationed himself with a spear in his left hand and a small wooden fish attached to a string in his right; the imitation fish being jerked up and down in the water attracted the larger ones, and they were easily speared.

I thought that what an Indian could do in that line, I could, and set about making my preparations. I whittled out a stick into the shape of a fish, shaping it as artistically as I could, and colored it by searing with a hot iron. In an excavation made for the purpose I poured melted lead to sink it, and after having placed in the head beads for eyes I had quite a natural looking fish, about four inches in length. Placing my spear head on a handle, I marched with them to the middle of Muskegon Lake, cut a hole in the ice, and erected a shelter by sticking poles in the ice and stretching a blanket over them. Everything being in readiness, I crawled into the hut, and lying flat on the ice dropped my "little pet"—as I called my little fish—and anxiously awaited the result. I was soon gratified by the appearance of a large fish that made a dart at my decoy. I hurled my spear at him, and—missed. And thus every few minutes for more than two hours I repeated the operation with the same results, when, mortified and angry, I returned, cold and hungry, to my solitary home and made a dinner of corn.

Brooding over my ill luck and awkwardness and almost discouraged, I concluded that "practice would make perfect," and that I would try again on the following day, which I did, and after an hour or so of unrewarded effort I succeeded in catching a large lake trout, with which I returned to my house and soon had boiling in my camp kettle; and never before or since did fish taste so good. After that I had no trouble in taking all the fish I wanted.

Every night a wolf came and devoured the remnants of the fish I had thrown out. I could see him through the cracks of my house, and could easily have shot him, but he was my only companion, and I laid awake at night awaiting his coming.

Thus I lived for thirty long, dreary, winter days, solitary and alone, never once during that time seeing a human being, and devoured with anxiety as to the fate of Dufrain and his men, whom I feared had met with some serious mishap, if, indeed, they had not been murdered. My anxiety for the last two weeks had been most intense, and at times I was almost crazy. I could not leave my goods, and knew not what I should do.

I looked upon the expedition as worse than a failure, and my first management of a trading house as a disastrous one. I thought that, should I live to return to

Mackinaw, I should be an object of ridicule among the traders, and have incurred the lasting displeasure of my employers, and this was to be the end of all my bright anticipations for the future. Oh, that I had been permitted to again accompany Mr. Deschamps and join my old companions at Beebeau's trading house.

My joy can be better imagined than described when, one morning, I discovered a party of men at the head of the lake coming toward me. I supposed them to be Indians, but was soon rejoiced to recognize among them Dufrain and his two companions. Having disposed of all their goods, and been successful in their trading, they had secured a large number of furs, and with the assistance of Indians, whom they had hired and equipped in snow-shoes, they had carried them on their backs. At the sight of the rich treasures they unloaded all my gloomy anticipations fled, and joy and satisfaction reigned in their stead.

The expedition had been one of great success ; the goods had all been disposed of, and in their place they brought the finest and richest of furs—marten, beaver, bear, lynx, fox, otter, and mink making up their collection.

Dufrain had a long account to give of trials, disappointments, and perseverance. He was ten days in finding the first band of Indians, and these had already been visited by an opposition trader, who cleared the camp of all the valuable furs and told the Indians that no trader would come to Muskegon. The Indians regretted his late arrival, as he was a great favorite with them.

Though in their progress thus far they had suffered greatly from want of provisions, and had progressed but slowly and with great fatigue owing to the depth of the snow, they determined to push on to other camps and dispose of their goods before the other trader should reach them. Having provided himself and party with provisions and snow-shoes, Dufrain despatched an Indian to me to tell me of his movements, and that he should be gone twenty days longer, and started on his way. We afterwards learned that after a half-day's travel the Indian injured his foot and was compelled to return to the camp, and thus I was left in ignorance of Dufrain's movements.

All was joy that night in our little household, the men as glad to return as I was to welcome them. I feasted them bountifully on corn soup and fish and listened to the recital of the incidents of their trip.

Another trip was decided on to go to the camp of some Indians he had heard of, but not seen, and who were in need of clothing, and had an abundance of furs. As time was very precious, the following day was devoted to selecting and packing goods and making preparations for departure. I decided to go with this expedition, though Dufrain remonstrated, and told me I could not stand the hardships of the journey; that having never traveled on snow-shoes I would have the *mal du raquette*, or become sick, and thus detain them; but to my mind anything could be easier endured than another month of such solitude as I had just passed through, and *mal du raquette* or sickness were nothing to be compared with what I had endured.

On the following morning we departed, leaving one man in charge of the house. Though my pack was only half as heavy as the others, the day was one of untold misery to me, never having walked in snow-shoes before.

6

The day was clear and cold, the country rough and hilly and covered with underbrush, and every few minutes I tripped and fell, and usually landed at full length and buried my face in the snow, from which I could not arise without assistance from the others. By noon I was completely exhausted, and my load was carried by one of the others; and though we had made an early start, when we camped at night we had traveled only about six miles.

Then came the preparations for the night's rest. The snow was about two feet deep, and shelter we had none. A place was selected by the side of a large fallen tree, the snow was scraped from the ground, and a place cleared of about six feet by ten, dry and green wood cut and piled up to the windward of the log, and a fire struck with flint and steel. Hemlock boughs were cut for bedding, and these covered with a blanket, to keep them down and in place; then the packs were placed at one end to protect our heads from the wind, and our beds were complete. During our march we had killed two porcupines, and these were dressed and toasted on sticks, and with our pounded parched corn made a very delicious supper. And as we had eaten nothing since early morning good appetites gave additional zest to the repast.

After supper, a smoke, and then to bed, all lying together on the hemlock beds, covered with the two remaining blankets, with our feet to the fire, which we replenished through the night. I slept but little, being kept awake by the aching of my legs, the muscles of which were badly swollen.

Before day all were up, and breakfast was made from the remnants of the previous night's supper, and by the time it was light we were ready to resume our journey.

I was so stiff and lame that I could scarcely walk, and Dufrain advised me to return, he offering to go part way with me, and there meet the other man, whom I should send from the house. I at first thought I would do so, but the recollection of the lonely month of anxiety I had passed there soon determined me to go on with the party, and all Dufrain's arguments failed to change my purpose. Every step caused me suffering, but as I warmed up the pain by degrees left me. I had caught the knack of throwing out the heels of my snow-shoes by a slight turn of the foot, and my falls were less fre quent, and when we camped at night we estimated that we had made during the day about three leagues or nine miles.

During the day we had cut from a hollow tree two rabbits, and these with corn furnished our supper. Our camp was made as on the previous night. In the morning we consumed the remainder of our stock o' corn, as we expected to reach an Indian camp by night, and made our usual early start.

Snow soon commenced falling, and continued hard all day, and as the weather had moderated the snow stuck to our shoes, making them heavy and the walking very tiresome ; we failed to find the Indians, and camped for the night with nothing to eat. The muscles of my toes were very sore, and on removing my moccasins and neips, I found my feet much swollen, and at the tops where the strap that held my snow-shoes was fastened. they were red and bruised, sure signs of "*mal du raquette.*" The morning found me in a sad condition. the swelling much increased, and the tops of my feet so sore that I could not bear my snow-shoes without great pain; still, on we went, I hobbling along as best I could. The snow still fell, and about noon we reached the Indian camp, and were provided with dinner by a squaw, and did ample justice to the bear meat and corn soup which she provided.

In the evening the Indians returned from hunting and trapping, bringing a good supply of furs, and the following forenoon was employed by them in selling their furs, and settling with Dufrain for the goods he had sold to them on a previous trip. We remained in this camp five days, and I was very kindly treated. The old squaw poulticed my feet with herbs, and for two days I practiced every hour or so on my snow-shoes, so that when we left these hospitable people I felt well and strong, and had no trouble in keeping up with the others, nor was I tired at night. We camped in the usual manner, having made fifteen miles that day.

Just at dark of the next day, as we were preparing our camp, we heard the bark of a dog, and knew the Indians were near; taking up our march, we soon reached their camp, where we remained for two days. A grand feast was prepared by the Indians, partly in honor of our visit, at which all the meat and broth set before us must be eaten, and the bones saved and buried with appropriate ceremonies, as an offering to the Great Spirit, that he might favor them in the hunt. The offering was a fat bear, over which a great pow-wow was first had by all the inmates of the lodges, after which it was carefully skinned, cut into small pieces, and put into the kettle in the presence of all.

During the cooking, speeches were made by some of the older Indians invoking the aid of the Great Spirit, and when cooked the meat was carefully removed from the kettles and distributed in wooden bowls to each individual present in such quantities as their age and capacity for eating would seem to warrant, and all receive their just proportion. Then the oil was skimmed off, and it and the broth divided in a like manner; a harangue was delivered by the head of the lodge, asking the Good Spirit to favor them in the chase and keep them well and free from harm ; and then the eating commenced.

I thought they had given me a larger portion than my age and capacity demanded, but Dufrain told me that I must eat all the meat and drink all the oil and broth. and leave the bones in my bowl ; that a failure to do so would be considered an insult to the Indians and an offense to the Great Spirit. "But," I said, "they have given me more than the others, and it is impossible for me to swallow it all." Dufrain replied: "They have given you the best portion as a compliment ; you must receive it, and eat and drink every bit and every drop, otherwise we shall have trouble." "Well, you must help me, then," I said. "No," he replied ; "I can't help you; each person must eat all that is given him, and will not be allowed to part with any portion of it; I am sorry for you, as well as for myself, and wish it had been a cub, instead of a fat bear, but I shall eat mine if it kills me."

It was between eight and nine o'clock at night, and the fire, which furnished the only light in the lodge, was low, and my location was in the back part of the lodge, where my movements could not be easily detected. I wore a French capote or hood, which suggested itself to my mind as being my only chance for disposing of a portion of the contents of my bowl, and I determined to attempt it. I felt that extreme caution was necessary, and no little dexterity required to slip the meat into the hood unobserved; but I took the first opportunity, and succeeded in safely depositing a piece without detection even by Dufrain, who sat next to me. I proceeded eating slowly, so that no notice might be taken of the diminished quantity in my bowl, and soon succeeded in depositing another piece, and then a third, and ended by eating the last piece. There still remained the oil and broth, and I feared that my now overburdened stomach could not stand this addition to its load. The grease had soaked through the cloth of my capote, and I could feel it trickling down my back, and I told Dufrain, in Indian, that I must go out, and asked him not to let my bowl be tipped over while I was gone. The Indians laughed, and I hastily made my exit, threw the pieces of meat to the dogs, and then, thrusting my fingers down my throat, endeavored to produce an eruption which should provide room for what I still had to swallow; failing in this attempt, however, I returned to my place in the lodge, and by persistent effort finally succeeded in swallowing the remainder.

The ceremony of gathering the bones was then gone through with by the head of the lodge picking them up very carefully and depositing them in a bowl, then another harangue, and we were left to chat and barter as suited us best.

From these Indians we learned of two camps situated in opposite directions, and from them engaged a guide to go with one of our men to one camp, and from there to another, we had before known of, and to return home, where we were to meet him. Dufrain, being well acquainted with the country, felt confident that he could go directly to the other camp in one day's travel, and I decided to go with him. When we lay down it was snowing hard, which continued through the night. We arose as usual before dawn of day, and partook of a nice dish of corn soup, which had been prepared for us by the good squaw in whose lodge we had slept, and as soon as possible started. The snow continued falling, and being soft stuck to our snow-shoes and made the traveling very hard and fatiguing, and by ten o'clock 1 discovered that my companion was in doubt as to our whereabouts, and at noon we halted near a large fallen tree to strike fire for a smoke. When I asked him if we should reach the camps that night, his reply was that we should have reached the river by that time, which would have been more than half way. He said he did not know where we were, the woods looked strange, but perhaps that was because there was so much snow on the trees. It had then stopped snowing, though with no appearance of clearing off.

Soon after we started the storm again commenced harder than ever, and I clearly saw that we were not going in the right direction, and ventured to tell Dufrain so. He was very passionate, and replied sharply that if I knew the way better than he I had better take the lead; thus rebuked, I followed on in silence. About four o'clock we found two tracks of snow-shoes. "Ah," said Dufrain, "you see we are right; these tracks are of to day; there is new snow on them; had they been of yesterday they would have been covered over so we could not see them; they were made by hunters from the camps this morning, but we can't go further than the river to-night. We will take the back tracks and they will lead us to the camps."

It so happened that during the earlier part of the day I had noticed a peculiar leaning tree, which was now in sight, and I told him we were lost, and would soon reach the log where we had stopped at noon. He could not believe that I was right, and on we went, but before dark he was convinced by our reaching the same log, and there we camped for the night. We both slept soundly, and arose refreshed. The snow still falling, we hesitated for some time, undecided whether to take our back track to the camp we had left, or to strike for the river in the direction we thought it to be. Knowing that if the snow continued, of which there was every prospect, our tracks would soon be obliterated, and Dufrain feeling confident that we could find the river and then know where we were, we decided to proceed. We traveled all day, and camped at night without having reached it. Again, another day's weary tramp with the same result, and Dufrain was willing to admit that he had no idea where we were. We still held our course, and again laid down to sleep, very tired and hungry.

The following day Dufrain became very weak, and was much frightened; still snowy, clouded, and dark; snow fully three feet deep. When we started the next morning, the clouds were breaking away, and by nine o'clock, the sun burst forth for the first time since we left the Indian camp. We then saw we were traveling a westerly course, and changed to the north. Dufrain was very weak, and our progress was necessarily very slow. Near a creek we found a thorn-apple tree, and removing the snow from the ground, found a few apples, which we devoured with a relish, and soon after struck the Muskegon River. Following up the river, we discovered on the opposite bank the poles of an Indian lodge, bark canoes, and a scaffold upon which was deposited matting for covering lodges. It was very cold, the river full of floating ice, and not fordable. Dufrain recognized the spot, and said that a half mile above were rapids, where the river could be forded. Having reached the rapids we crossed with great difficulty, the water in places being up to our waists, and the ice floating against us. When we reached the scaffold, our clothes were frozen stiff. We took down some of the mats, cleared the snow, and made a comfortable lodge, sufficiently large to shelter us.

Dufrain carried the flint, steel, and tinder in a bag, and after we had gathered wood for a fire, he discovered that he had lost it. We were indeed in a serious predicament, covered with ice, and shivering with cold; we supposed that we should certainly freeze to death. Dufrain abandoned all hope, and began to cross himself and say his prayers. I opened the bales of goods, and took from them what blankets and cloth they contained, cut more hemlock boughs, and took down more matting, and then we lay down close to each other, and covered up with the blankets and cloth. Soon the ice on our clothing began to thaw from the warmth of our bodies, and we fell asleep, never waking until sunrise.

We did not feel hungry, but were very weak, and neither felt inclined to move. We were dry and warm, and felt more like lying where we were and awaiting death than of making any further effort to save our lives. We knew the Indians could not be far away, and supposed we might soon find a snow-shoe path which would lead us to their lodges, but were not capable of making the effort to save ourselves. My own reflections of the responsibility resting upon me, and thoughts of my widowed mother, brother and sisters, finally nerved me to make an effort. I told Dufrain that we must get up and go to the camps, and that I would go and reconnoitre, find the path and return for him; to my great disappointment, however, I could find no snow-shoe tracks; but after careful search I discovered some small saplings broken off just above the snow, and could, by the feeling as I stepped, discover that there was a path under the newly fallen snow. I followed it for a short distance, when I saw a blaze on a tree, and knew that I was going in the right direction to find the camps. I returned for my companion, whom I found sleeping, and seeming not to have moved during my absence. With great difficulty I aroused him and put on his snow-shoes, and then, having placed both packs upon the scaffold, started on the march. I had much trouble in keeping the path, which I followed by the broken twigs and an occasional blaze on a tree, and our progress was very slow. About noon we struck a fresh snow-shoe track, and this gave me renewed energy, for I knew it had been made by a hunter from the Indian camps, and that by following the back track I should reach the lodges. Dufrain was not in the least moved by this good fortune; in fact, was stupid and inclined to stop, frequently crossed himself, while his lips moved as if in prayer, and it required much effort and persuasion on my part to get him to move slowly forward, he frequently protesting that he could not move another step.

Intent on my progress, and for a time forgetting my comrade, I advanced as rapidly as possible, and on looking around for Dufrain, I found he was not in sight; I deliberated a moment whether to return for him or continue on my way. My own strength was fast failing, and I feared that delay would be certain death. I resolved, however, to make a last effort, and turned back; I found him lying asleep in the snow. I tried to arouse him, but he would open his eyes but for a moment, and say, " I can't; leave me." Finding my attempts useless, I dug away the snow, wrapped him in his blanket, with mine over him, and left him.

I started forward conscious that I myself might soon be in the same condition, though determined not to give up while there was a hope. I felt no hunger, but was very weak; the perspiration ran from every pore, and at times everything seemed to waiver before me, with momentary darkness. I seemed almost to faint; still I moved on, reeling like a drunken man. Coming to new tracks, and hearing the barking of a dog, told me I was nearing a lodge, and gave me new strength to advance. Soon I was gladened by the glimpse of a lodge, and a few minutes more was seated on a bearskin within. It was a solitary hut on the bank of a creek, and in it was a middle-aged Indian, with his arm bandaged, and his squaw with three or four young children. I sat and awaited the usual custom of the Indians to set before a stranger something to eat, but seeing no move in that direction, I told the squaw that I was hungry and had not eaten for four days and nights. She exclaimed: "Nin guid buck-a-ta-minna baein" (we too are hungry; my husband broke his arm). She opened a sack and took out a small portion of pounded corn, which she stirred into a kettle of water and placed over the fire to boil, and soon as it was ready gave me a very small quantity, about half a pint, and replaced the kettle over the fire.

I supposed I was hungry, though I did not feel so, and supping a little from the wooden dish found it difficult to swallow. This frightened me and I lay down and slept.

I was awakened by the squaw, who gave me more soup from the kettle, which I ate with a relish and asked for more. "No," she said, "lie down and sleep, and I will awake you and give you more after awhile." This I did, and was awakened after dark refreshed but very sore and lame; took what soup was given me, and still wanting more; she refused me, saying, "after a little"; and that she knew best how to relieve me.

I noticed that the children frequently went out of doors, and that there was a look of anxiety on the countenances of both the Indian and squaw, which I thought was on my account; but asking. he replied that his oldest son went out early in the morning to try to kill something for them to eat, and they were fearful some accident had befallen him.

Up to this time I had not spoken of Dufrain, because I saw there was no one to go for him, and had there been, he could not have been reached before dark. The moon would rise about midnight, and then I had determined to ask the squaw to go with me for him, though I had no idea of finding him alive. They were well acquainted with him, and on my telling them of his situation the squaw parched what corn she had left, pounded it and got it ready, and we made preparations to go after him.

The squaw and her husband both thought that their son had gone to the river to see if the canoe and scaffold were safe, and that it was his track that I had followed to the camp. While we were discussing this idea, the dogs barked; the children ran out, and soon returned with the news that their brother had returned; and he soon entered, bearing a cub, whereat there was great rejoicing. It being the first of the larger animals he had ever killed, it must be offered to the Great Spirit as a thank offering, and the boy must fast for two days. The father sat up and beat a drum: the boy blackened his face, the bear was skinned, and preparations made for a feast, though fortunately the feast was not to be similar to the one I had attended shortly before, when all was to be eaten.

After hearing who I was, and that Jaco (Dufrain's Indian name) had been left behind, the boy volunteered to go with me in search of him : and when the moon rose, though I was scarcely able to move, we started. The Indian and his wife protested against my going, insisting that the boy and his mother could go without me, and I should gladly have consented to remain had I not known that if my comrade was found alive no one but me could get him to make an attempt to move.

The boy in his hunting had made a long detour, and on my describing the place where I had left Dufrain, he was able to reach it by a much shorter route than by following his tracks as I had done. In about an hour we reached Dufrain and found him apparently lifeless, but still warm. By much effort we aroused him so that he could speak, but he persisted in remaining where he was, said he was stiff and could not walk, and closed his

eyes and again dropped to sleep. It required our utmost
effort to raise him to his feet, and by short stages to
finally reach the camp just as the sun rose.

We made him as comfortable as possible, and by feeding him a little every few minutes revived him. His
feet and legs were badly swollen, so much so that I
was obliged to rip his leggins to get them off; his feet
were in a most terrible condition; the strings of his
snow-shoes had so bruised his toes that blood had oozed
out and completely saturated the neips; and, to add to
his misery, the poor fellow was ruptured, and it was
several days before I could replace the protruding parts.
He gained slowly, and it was a week before he could sit
up; and despairing of his restoration so as to be able to
bear the journey home, with the assistance of the boy
and his mother I constructed a *train-de-clese* on which
to remove him.

During my ten days' stay I had daily caught in traps
from one to a dozen partridges; and these, added to what
the boy had killed, furnished us a sufficiency of food,
though at times our rations were limited.

I finally got my sled fully rigged, though my friend
was still unable to sit up more than an hour at a time.
We had already spent more than ten days, and I felt
that I could remain no longer, and a decision must be
made, either to leave him and return for him, or draw
him on the sled to our home. The old Indian said we
might accomplish his removal; but he thought it extremely doubtful, the country being very hilly and
covered with underbrush. I left it to Dufrain to decide,
and as he chose to go, I started, with the young Indian
to assist me. We had a terrible journey over hills

and through thick undergrowth, and after three days of most severe toil reached our trading house, our invalid having borne the journey remarkably well.

The other party had only returned two days before, and all were anxious about us, and were about organizing an expedition to go in search of us. I was almost worn out from the hardships I had endured and from dragging my comrade.

Dufrain never left our cabin until we carried him to a canoe in the spring to start for Mackinaw. There was a light wind the day we started and the motion of the canoe caused vomiting, and before we could reach a harbor at White River he died, and we buried him in the bluff. He was very fond of card-playing during his life, and some Indians having camped on the bluffs where we buried him reported that at night they heard his voice calling out the name of the cards as he played them, "corno" (diamond), "cune" (heart), etc.; and though the river was a great resort for the Indians in the spring, where they used the peculiar white clay for washing their blankets, for years after they avoided it, believing it to be haunted.

We were among the very first of the traders to reach
Mackinaw, and after making my returns to Mr. Stewart
I was detailed for a time to the retail store. On Mr.
Matthews' return from Montreal I was assigned to duty
under him in the assorting and packing house, where
the business was conducted in the same manner as
previously described, and lasted until the last of July or
first of August.

My third winter was spent on the Kalamazoo River, in
Michigan, my trading house being on the north bank of
the river, and opposite the present city of Kalamazoo,
and for the first time I had full control of an "outfit."

My crew consisted of three Canadians, who were
accustomed to trading at that post, and an Indian
named Cosa, well and favorably known among the
Indians for bravery and intelligence. He had years
before abandoned hunting, preferring to engage for the
winter with some one of the regular traders as an
ordinary man or voyager. He received one hundred
dollars for his winter's service, which was considered
a high price for so short a time, and was as much as two

(96)

Canadians received for a whole year. But as he was perfectly familiar with the country, and well acquainted with the Indians, had a good reputation as a trader, and furnished two horses of his own, besides the services of his wife, I was glad to secure him even at that price.

This post was a pleasant one, though the hunting grounds were very much scattered, which made constant watchfulness and activity necessary to secure the furs and dispose of goods. The winter was one of great hardship, and my men were constantly out collecting furs, and occasionally I myself made a trip. Cosa sometimes took his wife with him in place of a man—she riding on one of the horses.

One evening on their return they reported having come across a camp of Indians on a branch of the Paw-Paw River, who had an abundance of furs and peltries, but Cosa, being out of goods, could only get from them what they already owed.

One of the Indians was very sick, and his friends had sent for a famous Indian doctor, who Cosa said always introduced his curing ceremonies by a drunken carousal. Cosa thought that we might get their furs if we could reach them ahead of the St. Joseph traders (who were connected with an opposition company), but he considered a little whisky absolutely necessary to secure their trade. I asked him to return to their camp in the morning with goods only, but he said he was very tired. I told him that it was but a short day's journey; that he could take his other horse that had been resting; to pack his goods, and that I would go with him, and leave his wife to keep house. He replied that it would be of no use without whisky, but that if I would take the

7

small keg he would go. He really needed two or three days' rest, and had the reputation of being a stubborn, fearless fellow, this reputation being confirmed by his many scars, and I did not like to command him to go. Heretofore he had shown a good disposition, was obedient and willing, and seemed to take more interest in the expedition, and had a greater desire for good results, than any of the other men, and I did not like to anger him if it could be avoided. I sought a private opportunity of consulting his wife, who confirmed all he had said, remarking, however, that she feared her husband could not refrain from joining in the ceremonies and getting drunk with the others. Her views decided me to accede to Cosa's wishes, and I said to him: "Now, Cosa, if we take the little keg and go to-morrow, will you promise to stick by me, and not taste a drop?" He promised, and that night two bales of merchandise, with the little two-gallon keg of highwines, watered one-third, were prepared; and at daylight in the morning the pony was brought from the woods, saddled and loaded, and we started, Cosa taking the lead.

I had also provided an empty one-gallon keg, and when about dark we arrived within hearing of the camp, I told Cosa that we would fill our small keg, mixed with half water, and hide the other, so that the Indians thinking that was all we had would be the sooner satisfied. To this he assented, saying it was wise. Though the highwines had been diluted one-third it was still quite strong. Having no funnel, how to further mix it was a dilemma, but we soon found a way. We would draw a mouthful from the larger keg and spit it into the smaller, and then take a mouthful of water and transfer it in the same way, Cosa and I alternating in the operation. It would have been wiser had I done this alone; but I found it burned my mouth badly and so permitted him to aid me, and thus gave him a taste, though I hardly think he swallowed any at the time. The transfer having been made, we hid the larger keg and proceeded to the camp, and to our disappointment found that Bartrand men had been there the day before and secured all the furs and peltries except a few remnants.

Some of the Indians had gone for the medicine man, while others had gone to Bartrand for whisky, which had been promised them in the trade. I would have returned had it been possible, but the horse was tired out, and the night very dark, so we accepted comfortable quarters which were tendered us, Cosa promising not to disclose the fact of our having whisky. The secret got out, however, and at early morn I was beset on every side, Cosa joining in the demand for the whisky.

There seemed to be no way but to sell a little, so I extorted a promise from Cosa to remain with me in the lodge and not to drink any, and commenced collecting what few furs they had in exchange for the whisky.

Cosa did not long keep his promise, but began to drink, and I saw the necessity of rehiding the larger keg before Cosa should reach the place. With the assistance of a squaw I changed the hiding place, first having refilled the smaller keg (which I again diluted), and hid it on the scaffold of the lodge I was in, and carefully covered it over. Cosa had told the other Indians I had more whisky, and joined them in urging me to give it to them, stating that if I did not they would go and take it; and being refused they went with him in search of it. Being disappointed in their attempts the Indians began to separate and go to their lodges, and soon all was quiet in the camp.

As my feet were wet I pulled off my moccasins and laid down in a wigwam with my feet to the fire. Cosa still importuning me for more drink, and I positively refusing, he, with two druken companions, after a long search, succeeded in finding the concealed keg. The squaw who assisted me in hiding the "fire water" had watched them, and quickly informed me of their discovery. I ran out into the snow barefooted, and succeeded in reaching the place before they could remove it from the scaffold. I told the two Indians that it was my property, and not theirs; that I should give them no more, and forbade them to touch it. They desisted, but Cosa, to show his independence, advanced to take the keg, when I seized him by the throat, threw him on his back, and placing my knees on his stomach, choked him so he could neither move nor speak, and held him thus until the squaw had removed the keg and again hidden it. I would not let him up until he promised me to lie down and sleep ; for a time he refused to promise; but as I only released my grip upon his throat long enough for him to answer, and then tightened it with renewed vigor, he was soon glad to promise, when I allowed him to arise and conducted him to my own comfortable quarters, covered him up, and lay down by his side.

Cosa was considerably injured, and after becoming sober slept but little. I myself kept wide awake until daylight, when I arose, got the pony from the woods, loaded him, and as soon as we had eaten our breakfast we departed homeward, picking up the keg on the way. Cosa was very hoarse from his severe choking, and very much mortified and humbled, and begged me not to tell what had taken place when we reached home; he was afterward very faithful and attentive to his duties.

In the month of November I made a trip to Chicago, and had a very delightful visit of a week in Mr. Kinzie's family, received my clothing which I had left there on my previous visit, and returned to my post.

During the fall of this year I made a *cache* in the sandhills at the mouth of the Kalamazoo River, in which I concealed many valuables, and early in the month of March following I took one of the men and went in a canoe for the articles. We found everything safe and in good condition, and having loaded them into the canoe started home. The weather was very severe for the season, and the snow still deep, which made our camping very unpleasant, and the current being swift, we had much difficulty in ascending the rapids, at the foot of which we had made our night's camp. I had collected some fine mink, otter, and other furs at two Indian camps on the route, and these, added to the articles taken from the *cache*, made a very valuable load.

I took my position in the bow of the canoe, leaving my man to steer. We had passed the rapids, but were still in a very strong current, when we came to a fallen tree lying in the river which formed a partial eddy. In pushing around the tree the strong current struck the boat sidewise, caused it to careen, and I lost my balance. To prevent the canoe from upsetting I allowed myself to go overboard and swam down the river;

the man quickly turning the head of the boat down stream, we both landed at the bottom of the rapids at the same time, where we found the fire of our previous camp still burning. After I had dried my clothing we again ascended, and reached home the following day without further mishap.

Nothing unusual occurred at my post that winter further than I have related.

I made a call on Rix Robinson, who was a trader on Grand River above Grand Rapids, also in the employ of the American Fur Company, and my nearest neighbor. It was in the month of January, a few days after a thaw which had flooded the river, and when I reached the South Branch of Grand River I found the bottoms flooded, but frozen hard enough to bear me up, the river very high and filled with floating ice, and no means of crossing, and I had either to return or swim for it. Though the day was very cold, I chose the latter, undressed, and having tied my clothing in as compact a bundle as possible, rested it on the back of my neck, holding it in place by a string between my teeth. I plunged in and soon landed on the opposite shore, and dressing myself as quickly as possible, I started on a run and soon became thoroughly warmed.

It was growing late, but being on the trail leading to Robinson's I felt sure of reaching his house, and arrived on the bank of the main river opposite to it about nine o'clock. I hallooed a number of times, and began to despair of being heard, and thought I should be compelled to camp for the night almost at the door of my friend. I gave my last and strongest yell, aroused a Frenchman, who came down to the shore and answered me, saying, in Indian, "Can't come over," and explaining that there was too much floating ice to cross. My answer, in French, telling who I was brought from him the reply, "Wait, we will come over": after a short time two men came for me in a boat, and I soon found myself beside a warm fire in my friend's cabin; supper was ordered, to which I did ample justice.

Robinson was much surprised at the account of my crossing the river. I spent a few days very pleasantly, and before leaving arranged with my host to wait at the mouth of the river for me on his way back to Mackinaw, so that we might proceed from there in company, I promising to be at the meeting place at an appointed day, not later than the tenth of May. Leaving Robinson's cabin at early dawn I reached my own post soon after dark, having traveled sixty miles. I had made a successful winter, and disposed of all my goods except a few remnants, and about the twentieth of April abandoned my post and descended the river, stopping for a day or two at the foot of the rapids, where a large number of Indians were assembled to catch sturgeon.

In due time I reached Grand River, where I found Mr. Robinson awaiting me, and after a rest of six or eight days we left for Mackinaw. We were among the first to arrive, and after settling my accounts, I was again detailed to the fur-packing house for the season.

I had received letters from my mother telling of her loneliness and of her great desire to see me, and felt very badly over the news these had conveyed; and when Mr. Crooks told me I was to again return to my post on the Kalamazoo River, I asked to be discharged, giving as a reason that my mother was a widow, and my brother and four sisters were all younger than myself, and needed my services and protection. I was then eighteen years old, and felt myself a man in all things. Mr. Crooks said the company could not spare me, and he thought I could serve my mother and family more acceptably by remaining; told me that he had corresponded with my mother, and when last at Montreal intended to have gone to Connecticut to see her, but had not the time, and by his arguments prevailed upon me to remain.

I expressed my desire to again go out with the Illinois "brigade," giving my reasons therefor; and these, aided by Mr. Deschamps' solicitations (he claiming that he had only consented to part with me for a year, expecting me to return and take charge of the post on the Illinois River), induced Mr. Crooks—though reluctantly—to give his consent to my going out with my old friend and comrade. In due course of time our "brigade" started, the twelve boats led by Mr. Deschamps and the old familiar boat song. I was again with my old companions, all of whom gave me a cordial welcome. Day after day we pursued our voyage, the ever monotonous row, row, being varied by no incidents of interest, until we reached Chicago. We had made an unusually quick trip, having been delayed by adverse winds but two or three days on the entire journey. Again I was rejoiced with a home in Mr. Kinzie's family, and remained there for several days, until the "brigade" again moved for the Illinois River.

The water in the rivers was unusually low this season, and in places the Desplaines could be crossed on foot without wetting the sole of the shoe; or, more properly speaking, the skin of the foot, as covering was out of fashion, or had not come in, at that time.

We were compelled to carry our goods and effects from the South Branch to the Desplaines on our backs, leaving our empty boats to pass through the usual channel from the South Branch to Mud Lake, and through that to the West End, and through the other channel. Having completed the portage to the Desplaines and encountered the usual fatigues in descending that river, without unusual delay or accident we reached Bureau Station, where I had passed my first winter. Mr. Beebeau was still in charge, though he was much more feeble than when I last saw him, nor had his temper and disposition undergone any change for the better, but on the contrary he was more irritable and disagreeable, if this was possible. My friend Antoine was also there and delighted to see me, and we spent many hours together, talking over old times and recounting our hunting experience of the winter of 1818-19. He had grown to manhood and was fully able to perform the duties and endure the hardships of a voyageur, in which capacity Mr. Deschamps engaged him for that post. He was greatly disappointed when he learned that I was not to winter with them but was to take the position of trader at a new post further down the river; he applied to Mr. Deschamps to be transferred to my post, but this was refused him, Mr. Deschamps stating to me that he feared I would not have the obedience from him that my position required, owing to our previous intimate relations in which he had been both my companion and equal. I saw the justice of this and acquiesced in his decision. Before parting, however, Antoine and I took a day's hunting together, tramping over ground which had become so familiar two years before, and recalling many pleasant incidents of those happy days.

After resting a few days, and selecting the goods and men to be left at that post, we proceeded on our way, making our next halt at Fort Clark (Peoria), where we found several families had located, among whom were Mr. Fulton, the first pioneer settler at that point, who still resides in that county ; a Mr. Bogardus, brother of General Bogardus, of New York, a highly intelligent gentleman, and his estimable and accomplished wife.

Two miles below, at a point now known as Wesley City, was Mr. Beason's post, and there we remained about one week, during which time I went almost daily to the fort.

WOLF STORIES.

A melancholy incident occurred there during the winter. On the river bottom opposite Beason's post were a half-dozen or more lodges of Pottawatomies. An aged squaw, accompanied by a young granddaughter, was returning from an absence from the camp, and when at Kickapoo Creek they were attacked by a large female timber wolf and her cubs. The little girl escaped, and running home reported to her brother, who immediately started to the old squaw's rescue. On reaching the place he found the wolves had killed his grandmother and were feasting upon her flesh. Though armed only with a tomahawk and knife, he boldly attacked the animals and succeeded in driving them away from her body, but not without being himself badly bitten, and,

indeed, I doubt not he would have departed for the
"happy hunting grounds" by the same route his grandmother had taken had he not been reinforced by his
friends, who had learned of his peril.

It is rarely that a wolf will attack a human being,
unless closely pressed or famishing with hunger. I remember that once when Noel Vasseur and myself were
eating our lunch at Blue Island, while our horses were
grazing, a wolf came so close to us that Vasseur toma-
hawked him.

Another time, Jacques Jombeaux and myself had
camped for the night, and before lying down I went to
look after my horse, which I had spanceled on the
prairie. I found him feeding quietly, and returning, I
noticed what I supposed to be an Indian dog following
me. I called and whistled to him, but he paid no attention to the noise. When I reached the camp I told
Jacques that there was a camp of Indians near, as I
had been followed by one of their dogs, and that he
must hang up the provisions. He hung them on a
sapling close by our camp fire. We were lying with
our feet close to the fire when my supposed dog came
up and put his forefeet on the sapling in his efforts to
get our meat. The light of the fire showed him to be
a prairie wolf, and enabled Jacques to shoot him with
his rifle.

I knew of an Indian who was treed by a pack of
wolves, and there kept for eighteen or more hours,
until his comrade, becoming alarmed at his absence,
found and relieved him.

We left Beason's and proceeded on our way to other
stations down the river. Mr. Deschamps decided to

establish a new post at the mouth of Crooked Creek, and to locate me in charge. We soon agreed upon the spot on which to build my house, and my outfit having been unloaded Mr. Deschamps proceeded on his way.

We first constructed a pen of logs, the sides of which were about six feet high, within which was packed my goods; these were covered with sails and tarpaulins. Our camp was made on the south side of the inclosure, both for convenience and the better protection of the goods. These arrangements having been completed we proceeded immediately to build a good-sized trading house.

Before reaching this place I had felt symptoms of ague, loss of appetite with slight chills; still I managed to keep up, and my house-building progressed so well that by the time of Deschamps' return it was up and the store part covered, so that the goods could be moved into it. Mr. Deschamps thought my symptoms denoted bilious fever and prescribed for me accordingly.

My fever continued to increase, and I became very sick, was unable to sit up, and daily grew worse.

Two Frenchmen, who had been shooting geese and swans at Portage de Sioux, came down the Illinois River in a large pirogue, on their way to St. Louis to market their game. Though their boat was heavily laden, by promising to pay for the game they would be compelled to leave to make room for me, and also to pay liberally for my passage, I succeeded in persuading them to take me as a passenger to St. Louis, where I felt compelled to go to consult a physician, and their arrival seemed providential.

While the men were eating I made preparations for my

departure. Calling my interpreter, I told him of my determination, and instructed him that should I fail to return by a certain day he should send word to Mr. Deschamps and ask for orders. My men went to work with a will moving and repacking the game so as to give sufficient room for me in the boat without leaving any part of the load, and I was carried and placed in the boat, in as comfortable a position as could be found.

The wind was from the south, and the river very rough; the motion of the boat caused me to vomit excessively and I soon became unconscious. The men carried me along until they came to a settler's cabin near the bank of the river, and supposing me to be dying, took me ashore, left me there, and pursued their journey. I do not know how long I was unconscious, but when I awoke I found myself in bed, while a young girl was sitting by fanning me. She jumped up and called her mother, who coming in, cautioned me not to get excited, gave me some tea, and while I was drinking it told me where I was and how I came there. From that time I improved rapidly, and in the course of a week or ten days I was able to start on foot for my trading house, about thirty-five miles distant, which I reached in two days, much to the joy and astonishment of my men. I can not conceive why I have lost from my memory the name of those hospitable people, who took me into their house and nursed me so kindly, but so it is, and their name I can not remember. I never saw them but once afterward.

I found my house was nearly completed. I had a good appetite, and increased daily in strength, so that I was soon able to hunt on the river bottom, ranging two or three miles from the house. One bright November morning I started out for a turkey hunt, and soon came across some fresh horse tracks which I supposed were those of Indian ponies, and gave them no further thought; but at a little creek I saw the tracks again, and in a muddy spot I noticed the fresh impression of a horse-shoe, and so followed their trail, and after about a mile travel came up with the riders and found them to be Mr. John Wood and Mr. Tilden, on their way to the military tract to locate soldiers' land-warrants. I thought they were lost (though the Governor always denied it), as they were not in the direct course, and their tracks made a strange circuit for persons knowing their whereabouts. I led them to my house and prepared for them the best meal in my power, of which they ate very heartily and with decided relish. Governor Wood has often told me that it was the best meal he ever ate. I am quite willing to believe it was good, and flatter myself that the cooking I did in those days, if not in the style of a French cook, was, for plain food, deserving of great praise. I have never tasted of any roast turkey that seemed to me so excellent as those fat wild ones killed and prepared by my own hands.

I used to hang them in front of my large fire place suspended by a string, and gently turn them with a long stick until they were nicely browned, and then with fat raccoon or bear meat boiled, I had a dinner fit for a king. My new found friends left me in the afternoon though I tried hard to detain them; like most of the enterprising "Yankees" of those early days they could not be stayed. Both of these gentlemen located in Quincy, Illinois, became prominent citizens, and finaly died there. Mr. Wood was at one time Governor of the State of Illinois, and I ever considered him as one of my warmest friends.

My house was soon completed and furnished with floor, three-legged stools, table, and bunks, all made of puncheons. It was lighted by a window in the south end, made of two sheets of foolscap paper nicely greased; and with a fine large clay chimney that would take in a six-foot log, I felt that the cold or storms of winter could have no terrors for me.

I was now fully recovered in health, and all my care and anxiety was for the success of the winter's trade.

The Indians were Kickapoos and Delawares, and being a stranger among them, I was forced to depend on my interpreter, who was well acquainted with them, to know whom to trust.

It was our custom to give the Indian hunters goods on credit, in the fall of the year, so that they might give their whole time to the hunt, and, indeed, it would have been difficult, if not impossible, for them to hunt without the necessary clothing, guns, and ammunition. The conditions of this credit were that these advances should be paid from the proceeds of their first winter's hunt, but should they fail to pay, after having devoted all their furs for the purpose, and shown a disposition to act honestly, the balance was carried over to the next year, but this balance was seldom paid. The debtors reasoned that, having appropriated the entire proceeds of their season's hunt to the liquidation of their indebtedness, it was the fault of the Great Spirit that they had not been able to pay in full, and so they considered the debt canceled. We were very careful who we trusted.

(112)

We satisfied ourselves first, that the person's intentions were honest, and that he was industrious and persevering; and, second, that he was a skilled hunter and trapper, and knew where to find game in abundance. If he lacked in these qualifications he was deemed unworthy of credit, at least to a large amount.

I was applied to for credit by an Indian whom my interpreter said "never paid," or if he paid at all, it was only a portion of his indebtedness. I accordingly refused him, at which he was greatly angered and threatened revenge.

One morning shortly after, I was sitting alone before the fire in my cabin, on a three-legged stool made of puncheons, reading a book, when the Indian returned and stole softly into the room, and up behind me, with his tomahawk raised to strike me. I did not hear him, but saw his shadow, and looking up quickly saw him, and threw up my left arm just in time to arrest the blow. The handle of the tomahawk striking my arm, it was thrown from his hand and fell on the floor close to the fire-place. The corner of the blade cut through my cap and into my forehead—the mark of which I still carry—while my arm was temporarily paralyzed from the blow. I sprang to my feet just as he reached to his belt to draw a knife, and throwing my arms around his body, grasped my left wrist with my right hand, and held him so firmly that he could not draw his knife. I allowed him to throw me down on the floor, and roll me over and over in his exertions to liberate himself and reach his knife, while I made no exertions except to keep my grip. I bled profusely from the wound on my forehead, and my eyes were frequently blinded by the blood, which I wiped off as well as I could on his naked body. It was fully five minutes before my arm began to recover sensitiveness, and a much longer time before I recovered its full use.

My grasp was weakening, yet I clung on afraid to trust to my lame arm. My opponent was breathing very heavily, and I knew he was exhausting his strength in his efforts to rid himself of my embrace, while I was saving mine. When my arm had sufficiently recovered, and we had rolled up to where the stool lay, I let go of him, and seizing the stool struck him a stunning blow upon the head, which I followed up with others on his head and face, until he showed no further signs of life, when I seized him by his long hair and dragged him out of doors, whooping for my men, who soon made their appearance. Just then his squaws appeared on the scene. He had come on his pony, telling them he was going to kill Hubbard, and they had followed on as rapidly as they could on foot. They bathed his head with cold water, and, greatly to my relief, soon restored him to consciousness. I reflected that I had punished him too severely, and regretted that I had done more than to strike him the first blow and then disarm him. My men were greatly alarmed, and especially so was my interpreter, whom I sent to the chief of the band to explain the case.

The chief returned with my man and blamed me for injuring him so severely, thinking it would result in his death. However, he used his influence with the band in my favor, telling them the goods were mine, and that I had a perfect right to refuse to sell them on credit and to defend myself when attacked, and they soon separated for their winter hunting grounds, much to my relief.

The injured Indian did not recover so as to do any hunting that winter, and occasionally sent me a message demanding pay for his injuries, which I positively refused, much to the dissatisfaction of my confidential man.

The winter passed and we were ready to break up, daily expecting orders from Mr. Deschamps to start on the return trip to Mackinaw. The Indians had returned from their hunting grounds and were camped some five or six miles from us. They had mostly paid up, though the winter had not been a successful one for them.

The chief was a young man, and had become very friendly to me. He advised me to give presents to the Indian I had injured; but I still persisted in my refusal, determined to risk the consequences rather than to pay a man for attempting to kill me. This was reported to my enemy, who had fully recovered his strength, and exasperated him still further. One morning he came with two of his friends, all with blackened faces, a token of war, and demanded of me pay for his injuries. I again refused, telling him that it was his own fault; that he came upon me stealthily, and would have killed me had I not discovered him just in time to save myself. While thus talking I heard the tramp of horses, caused by the arrival of the chief and others of the band, who, hearing of his intention to seek revenge, had hastened to try to effect a friendly arrangement.

On entering I stated to the chief the demand made upon me, and my refusal, and that now he and his friends had come like men, and not like squaws, and that this time I was prepared for them.

"I came," I said, "among you with goods for your accommodation; trade was my object, and I have as much right to do as I please with my goods as you have with the pony you ride. You would not allow any one to take him without your consent; and, should any one attempt to take him by force, would you not defend yourself? Or would you, like a coward, give him up? Say, would you?" "No," he replied. "Neither did I, nor will I. I am very sorry for what I did—I mean, the result, causing the loss of his winter's hunt; but I will not pay him for it." The chief said to them, "The trader is right; the goods were his; he would not trust because our friend (pointing to the interpreter) said you never paid. We all know that is true." After a moment of silence the Indian extended his hand to me, which I took. "Now," I said, "we are friends, and I wish to give you some evidence of my friendship, not to pay you, but only as a token of my good will." We all had a smoke, and I presented him with articles he most needed, much to his surprise. And so that difficulty was ended, much to the satisfaction of my men, who were fearful that great trouble would result from it.

About ten days after the above settlement I received orders from Mr. Deschamps to vacate my post and join the "brigade" at Beason's post. There we remained a week or more, during which time I formed an intimate acquaintance with the settlers at Peoria.

About the first of April we resumed our journey toward Mackinaw, proceeding leisurely, and reaching Chicago in due season, where, as usual, I found a warm welcome from the Kinzie family and officers of the fort. A week or ten days was thus joyfully spent, and I deeply regretted the day of our departure.

Coasting, as before, the east shore of Lake Michigan,

we arrived at Mackinaw early in June. On the sixth of
that month I was present when Alexis St. Martin was
shot, and am probably the only living person who witnessed the accident.

The late Major John H. Kinzie had charge of the
American Fur Company's retail store at Michilimackinac.
I was in the habit of assisting him occasionally when a
press of customers needed extra clerks. The store comprised the ground floor near the foot of Fort Hill, on the
corner of the street and the road leading up to the fort.
The rear part of the store was underground, built of stone,
which is still standing.

This St. Martin was at the time one of the American
Fur Company's engagees, who, with quite a number of
others, was in the store. One of the party was holding a
shot-gun (not a musket), which was accidentally discharged, the whole charge entering St. Martin's body.
The muzzle was not over three feet from him—I think not
over two. The wadding entered, as well as pieces of his
clothing; his shirt took fire; he fell, as we supposed,
dead.

Dr. Beaumont, the surgeon of the fort, was immediately sent for, and reached the wounded man within a
very short time—probably three minutes. We had just
got him on a cot and were taking off some of his clothing.

After Dr. Beaumont had extracted part of the shot,
pieces of clothing, and dressed his wound carefully—
Robert Stewart and others assisting—he left him, remarking, "The man can't live thirty-six hours; I will come
and see him bye and bye." In two or three hours he
visited him again, expressing surprise at finding him
doing better than he anticipated.

The next day, I think, he resolved on a course of treatment, and brought down his instruments, getting out more shot and clothing, cutting off ragged ends of the wound, and made frequent visits, seeming very much interested, informing Mr. Stewart in my presence that he thought he could save him.

As soon as the man could be moved he was taken to the fort hospital, where Dr. Beaumont could give him better attention. About this time, if I am not greatly mistaken, the doctor announced that he was treating his patient with a view to experimenting on his stomach, being satisfied of his recovery. You know the result.

I knew Dr. Beaumont very well. The experiment of introducing food into the stomach through the orifice purposely kept open and healed with that object, was conceived by the doctor very soon after the first examination.

My duties in the assorting and packing warehouse that summer gave me but little time for recreation. In fact, until after six o'clock in the evening, I had no time to myself, and I frequently worked until midnight. Sunday afternoon was the only time at which I felt fully at leisure to visit my friends, and that was passed either at Mrs. Fisher's, Mrs. La Fromboise's, Mrs. Mitchell's, Mr. Davenport's or Mr. Dousman's, at any of which places I was ever a welcome visitor. Thus was completed the fourth year of my life as an Indian trader.

Early in the fall I left Mackinaw in the usual way for my fifth winter in the Indian country. By request of Mr. Crooks we invited a gentleman to accompany us, who desired to visit Southern Illinois. He was a gentleman of intelligence; in figure, tall and gaunt, and possessed of one of those inquisitive minds which ever denotes the genuine "Yankee." He was continually asking questions and wanting an explanation of every thing he saw or heard, and did not hesitate to pry into our private affairs and investigate our personal characteristics. He was exceedingly awkward in his positions in the boat and camp, and could never accustom himself to sitting "tailor fashion." His limbs and body were in a continuous change of "sprawl," and at times interfering with the motions of the oarsman and forcing an involuntary "sacre" from the *voyageurs*, who were proverbial for politeness and natural grace. To them he became alternately an amusement and an annoyance, and as he could not understand their language, numerous jokes were indulged in at his expense, and he was nicknamed "La Beauté."

At one time we were caught in a wind-storm which compelled us to land and draw our boats up on the beach. On such occasions it was customary for the men to carry the *Bourgeois* ashore on their back. Our guest straddled the shoulders of one of the men, who purposely fell, taking care that his rider should fall under him and become completely submerged, at the same time exclaiming, "Mon Dieu, monsieur, excusez moi," and quickly helping him to his feet continued his apologies. Seeing our friend completely drenched, the water dripping from his clothing, and his hat floating off on the waves while the *voyageur* seemed so sincere in his apologies, was too much for our silent endurance, and we all broke out into peals of laughter, in which our dripping passenger heartily joined. His company was agreeable to all save the *voyageurs* and he was always invited to choose which boat he preferred to ride in for the day.

We reached Calf River without any particular incident, where we camped, and on the following morning I invited our friend to walk with me to the top of "Sleeping Bear," and join the boats when they reached its base. "Sleeping Bear" was a high bluff, six or eight hundred feet above the lake. With the exception of a small clump of trees, its top was a naked plain of sand without vegetation of any kind. Its lake front was very steep, and it was with great difficulty and exertion that it could be ascended; the loose sand into which one sank several inches at each step, slid downward carrying one with it, so that progress was slow and tedious. To *walk down* was impossible unless one went backward, and in a stooping posture. It was real sport to go down by quick successive jumps, and fortunate was the individual who could accomplish it without losing his balance, falling over and rolling to the bottom, where he arrived with mouth, nose, and ears filled with the fine shifting sand, though there was little or no danger of anything more serious.

We reached the summit, and after viewing the lake and country, and our boats having arrived at the base, I said to my friend, "We must descend by jumps; take as long leaps as you can, and *don't stop;* follow me"; and with a loud "whoop" to attract the attention of the boatmen, I went down by quick jumps, but before reaching the bottom heard the shouts of the *voyageurs*, and though I could not look back, I knew full well the cause. When I had arrived at the bottom, I looked back and saw my companion struggling and rolling, while the sand flew in every direction. He landed close to my feet pale and frightened, but otherwise unharmed. The men screamed with laughter, much, as I thought, to the annoyance of our passenger, though he made no complaint, and having been brushed off, took his seat in the boat, and we proceeded on our way.

This incident served for a standing joke, and many times was the laughter renewed when the ludicrous affair was again presented to our minds. Although we had enjoyed ourselves so much at his expense, we learned to like him for his many good qualities, and when we parted with him at Peoria, it was with many and sincere regrets.

Our trip was a tedious one, we being kept many days in camp by heavy adverse winds. We were nearly a month in reaching Chicago, where, as usual, I was welcomed by my friends, the Kinzies. who, with Dr. Wolcott, rendered me many kind services.

At Chicago I found Pierre Chouteau, Jr., of St. Louis, whose acquaintance I had formed several years before, and who now proposed that I should enter their employ at the expiration of my engagement with the American Fur Company; during my two weeks' stay we became very intimate. The officers of the fort were good companions, and I passed much of my time with them, and very pleasantly, and much regretted the time of parting.

We encountered the usual trials and hardships between Chicago and Starved Rock, and in due season arrived at Bureau Post, where I had passed my first winter, and Mr. Beebeau having died since our departure the previous spring, I was placed in charge.

An opposition trader named Antoine Bourbonais, who was supplied with goods from St. Louis, had located there. He was a large, portly man, and for one of his years, was very energetic, and was an old, experienced trader. Mr. Deschamps told me of his virtues and failings, warned me of his tricks, and cautioned me as to my intercourse with him. My old Indian friends, Wa-ba and Shaub-e-nee, were also here to welcome me.

It was late in the season when we arrived, and Bourbonais had already been located for more than a month, and in him I found a strong competitor. He was possessed of a "foxy" sharpness, was fond of his cups, and when under their influence, inclined to be quarrelsome. I was as friendly toward him as could be expected, and while we treated each other with respect, we watched each other closely, each striving to supply the best hunters with their winter outfits, and in this we exercised all the secresy and strategy in our power; but after the Indians had received their supplies and departed to their hunting grounds, our intercourse was very friendly.

The time soon arrived when we were to visit the camps of the Indians in the interior and endeavor to secure their furs, collect the amounts with which they had been credited, and sell to them the goods which we carried with us. Bourbonais had five or six horses, while I had none, which of course gave him a great advantage, as he could pack his goods onto the horses, and return with his furs in the same manner, while I depended on the backs of my men.

With a light load, my men could travel as fast as the horses, that depended for their subsistence on foraging on the half-dead grass of the bottom lands.

To know when and where an expedition was to go was very necessary, and every strategy was resorted to, and considered perfectly fair, to conceal these facts from each other. As a consequence, we watched each other constantly, sometimes quarreled, though never coming to blows, quickly becoming friendly again, and frequently telling how one had outwitted the other in the course of trade. We both had a laborious and exciting winter, though neither cut the prices on leading articles.

At one time, I learned from an Indian that Bourbonais was packing up some bales of goods, and we had noticed that he had gathered his horses in from their feeding grounds ostensibly to salt them, all of which led me to suspect that an expedition was being fitted out, and I detailed a man to watch. Just before daylight, my man reported that two horses were loaded with goods and another saddled, which convinced me that Bourbonais was himself going, as he usually rode, being too clumsy to walk. To ascertain where they were going, I hired an Indian, who happened to be at my house, to follow at a distance, pretending to hunt, until they should leave the timber and take their course over the prairie.

In the meanwhile, I prepared three bales of goods, of twenty-five pounds each, and detailed three of my men to carry them, giving Noel Vasseur charge of the expedition, with instructions to take the track and overtake Bourbonais that day, and, if possible, pass him without being seen ; but if unable to do that, to camp with him for the night. The Indian returning, reported the course the expedition had taken, and we then knew that they were bound for one of two hunting bands, but which one we could not tell.

Vasseur started with his men and soon came in sight of Bourbonais and his party, but being on the open

prairie could not pass them without being noticed, and
so decided to overtake them by dark, and camp with or
near them. Bourbonais, finding his secret discovered,
extended his usual hospitality to Vasseur and party, and
after they had finished their suppers, offered them a dram,
which was gladly accepted. Vasseur and he chatted and
drank, until by daylight the old man was dead drunk.
Vasseur had gained a knowledge of their destination,
and with his companions started for the Indian camps,
knowing full well that Bourbonais could not get sobered
up and catch his horses on the range in time to overtake
them. By hard marching Vasseur found the camp, collected some of the debts, and bought all the surplus furs
and peltries by the time Bourbonais reached the camp.
The old man was much mortified and angered when he
discovered how he had been outwitted, but soon got over
it, and together he and Vasseur, visited the other band,
collected their credits, and returned home. In this manner the winter was passed.

On Mr. Deschamps' return he bought Bourbonais'
furs, engaged him in the service of the American Fur
Company, and he was afterwards stationed at Kankakee,
where he died. Mr. Deschamps was well satisfied with the
result of my winter's trade, it being much better than he
had anticipated. The season had been an unusually good
one, and we had accumulated more furs and peltries
than our boats could carry up the Desplaines River, and
I was accordingly dispatched with four boat loads to
Chicago; these I stored with Mr. John Crafts, and
returned to the "brigade," when we all moved forward
on our annual return to Mackinaw. A portion of our furs
were shipped from Chicago, for the first time, in a small
schooner which had brought supplies for the garrison.

In the month of March (1823), I had occasion to go alone to see some Indians who were camped at "Big Woods" on Fox River, in Du Page County, west of Chicago.

After I had transacted my business with them, and the evening before my return home, an Indian who belonged to another band, which was camped about ten miles distant, came into the wigwam where I was, and said he was going to my trading house. I gave him some supper, and told him I should start in the morning and that he could accompany me, to which he assented. We started in the morning as early as we could see to travel, and found the ground soft and muddy, and the walking hard and tedious, but I noticed that my companion walked very fast.

About noon he stopped to smoke, but having made up my mind that he wanted to race, I kept on as fast as possible and got a long distance ahead of him.

When I reached the Illinois River above Hennepin, and opposite my trading house, I discovered that the canoe which I had left there had been stolen. The bottom lands were overflowed from the river to the bluffs. I finally got upon a log, and by pulling on the bushes and pushing with a stick, managed to propel it to the bank of the river.

I shouted to my men, and waited a long time for them to answer, but receiving no response, 1 jumped in and swam across, reaching my house about dark.

The following morning I sent my men back across the river to look for the Indian; they found him with a party of others on horseback, very much chagrined and disappointed at his defeat. I then learned that the band which I had visited had made a wager with the band to which my companion of the day before belonged that I could outwalk any one they could produce, and they had planned the race without intending that I should know of it.

The distance walked that day is seventy-five miles, in a direct line, according to the present survey. I suffered no inconvenience from it, though the Indian was very lame for a day or so.

Some have doubted that I could have walked so great a distance, but I was then young and in my prime, and had long had the reputation among the Indians of being a very rapid traveler, and had, in consequence, been named by them Pa-pa-ma-ta-be, "The Swift Walker."

It was a well-known fact, at that time, that Pierre Le Claire, who carried the news of the war of 1812, was sent by Major Robert Forsythe to his uncle, Mr. John Kinzie, at Chicago, and that he walked from the mouth of St. Joseph River around Lake Michigan to Chicago, a distance of ninety miles, in one continuous walk.

He arrived at Mr. Kinzie's, ate his supper, and crossed over the river to report to the officers of Fort Dearborn, before nine o'clock at night, having started before daylight from St. Joseph river.

We made our usual stay in Chicago, I among my good friends, and without incident worthy of note, arrived in due season at Mackinaw. I was placed in entire charge of the receiving of furs, assorting and packing them for shipment. It was a full two months' work, of hard, fatiguing duty. All the furred skins, except muskrats and wolves, had each to pass my inspection, and when examined, all the finer, fancy furs, were to be assorted as to shades of color, as well as to fineness of fur. I was furnished with assistants who, after I had assorted the furs, counted and delivered them to the packers to press, tie, mark, and store, ready for shipment, one hundred *voyageurs* being detailed for this duty. The roll was called regularly at six o'clock in the morning, and with the exception of one hour's intermission at noon, our labors were incessant until six at night.

After the day's labor was ended, I was required to make up an account showing the total of that day's work. The statement for each outfit was kept separate on my packing-house book, from which it was drawn off by myself or one of my assistants, and filed with the book-keeper in the general office.

Complaints were frequently made that I assorted too closely, and not unfrequently Mr. Stewart would himself re-assort, with the manager of the " brigade," who was interested in making his returns appear as large as possible, but usually my assorting was approved. I made it an invariable rule never to open and re-assort a pack.

The different outfits were required to furnish me a list of their packs, their contents, and number of skins unassorted. One of my assistants opened each pack and counted the skins, and if found to be short it was his duty to notify the chief of the "outfit" or his representative, who was usually present, in order that his count might be corrected, and my returns when made agree with his, and errors and dissatisfaction be thus prevented.

I was glad to reach the close of this summer's duties. It was very fatiguing work to stoop over and assort from morning until night. I had no time for rest or recreation until the last skin was in pack ready for shipment.

The packs were very neatly put up in frames, nearly square in form, and intended to weigh about one hundred pounds each. It required much practice before the men selected for that purpose became experts. The skins must be placed in proper positions, evenly distributed, so as to make the pack press equally, the ends built up straight, so as to show no depressions or elongations, and a failure in either of these particulars necessitated repacking.

The different kinds of skins were packed in different ways, each kind having its own peculiar manner of folding, while all packs were required to be of the same size ; and when taken from the press, they resembled huge reams of paper, so even and uniform were the ends and sides. We used screw presses, worked by hand, and if a pack came from the press without filling all the requirements, it was repacked and repressed. Each pack was then numbered, and an invoice of its contents made, which received the same number.

Adjoining the warehouse was a large yard, into which the packs were received when brought from the Indian country and in which they were opened. Each skin was thoroughly beaten to rid it of bugs and dust, and if damp it was dried, and then carried into the warehouse for assorting, counting, and packing. About the middle of August my work was completed, and I was at liberty to use my time as I chose. I employed it in visiting my friends, and thus improved it to the last moment. Again we were ready to depart on our monotonous lake voyage, coasting as usual the east shore of Lake Michigan, and meeting with no incident worthy of mention until we reached St. Joseph, where we were detained for several days by head winds. My destination had been decided by Mr. Deschamps to be the Iroquois country. We knew that it was but a short distance from a bend of the St. Joseph River to the Kankakee River, and I determined to endeavor to pass my boats and goods overland to the Kankakee, and thus save the remainder of the journey to Chicago, as well as the delays and hardships of the old route through Mud Lake and the Desplaines.

From Mr. Burnett, who lived a little more than a mile from where we were then camped, I learned that the Indians near Bartrand trading house had ponies on which my goods could be packed, and he thought the Indians would also undertake to pass my boats across, suggesting that by hitching the tails of the ponies to the boats they could be made to help considerably.

Having concluded a favorable arrangement with the

9

Indians. I undertook the venture, telling Mr. Deschamps that if I failed. I would return and overtake him at Chicago.

I selected my men, among them being Noel Vasseur, in whom I had the utmost confidence, wrote a letter to my good friends, the Kinzies, telling them of the change in my plans, and that I would visit them after I got settled in my winter quarters. I sent also to Mr. Kinzie my best clothes for safe keeping.

Everything being in readiness, I started early on the following morning, and soon passed an old Jesuit mission, afterwards occupied by Mr. Coy. We halted a short time at Bartrand's, and from him I received full information about the Kankakee River, and he tendered me every assistance in his power in making the crossing. Proceeding to the place of leaving the St. Joseph I met the Indians with their ponies, and following the suggestion of Mr. Burnett, cut poles and lashed them across the boats, which had been unloaded, at the bow and stern. We then wove and tied the ponies' tails securely to the poles at the stern, and tied their heads to the ones at the bow. In order that the boats might move more easily, we placed rollers under them, and then the Indians and squaws commenced urging the ponies forward. For some time they were awkward and stubborn, some would pull, while others would not, but by patience and perseverance, the men also pulling, we finally got them started and advanced for a hundred or more yards, when the ponies came to a dead stand. We again applied the rollers and the muscles of the men, and succeeded in making another start, and the ponies becoming accustomed to the work, soon got so they would make a quarter of a mile at a stretch, and in this manner we passed our boats over and launched them into the Kankakee. Repacking our goods and loading them into the boats, we were soon ready to embark. We found the Kankakee narrow and crooked, with sufficient water to float our boats, but with very little current.

Our progress under oars was at the rate of fifty or sixty miles a day, and we met with no obstacles until we reached the upper rapids or shoals, where the village of Momence is now located.

From that point, shallow water continued at intervals until we reached the mouth of the Iroquois River, which river we ascended to a trading house, located a short distance below the present village of Watseka, which was our destination.

The Messrs. Ewing, then of Ft. Wayne, had a trading house further up the river, and opposite the present village of Iroquois. This house was in charge of one Chabare, and it was for the purpose of opposing him that I had been detailed. Our house was soon put in a habitable condition, and my first leaving it was for the purpose of visiting Mr. Chabare, with whom, during the entire winter, I continued on friendly relations.

Having made friends with the Indians, to whom I gave liberal credits, and having noted where they severally intended making their hunting camps, I slipped away for a week's visit to Chicago, principally to see my good friends the Kinzies, having as usual a very agreeable visit, and promising to return at Christmas time, which, however, I was prevented from doing.

In the spring I had but a handful of goods left, and the result of my winter's business was quite satisfactory to both Mr. Deschamps and the managers of the Company at Mackinaw.

Before Mr. Deschamps' arrival I abandoned my post and went to Chicago, there to await him and the brigade. It was about a month before they came, at which delay I was well pleased, as I passed my time with the family of Mr. Kinzie, who, with Dr. Wolcott and the officers of the fort, made my visit very pleasant. I much regretted leaving, and reluctantly parted from my friends, uncertain whether I should ever see them again, as my term of service was about expiring.

I had not settled in my mind what was my duty and interest. My inclination led me to my mother, who was struggling to support her four young daughters. My young brother Christopher had obtained a position in the hardware store of Henry King, in New York, but was receiving only his board for his services.

In my uncertainty what course to pursue I resorted, as was my custom, to Mr. Kinzie for advice, and also consulted the Indian agent, Dr. Wolcott, who was from Middletown, Conn., and knew my mother well. It was now five years since I parted from my loving Christian mother and my sisters and brother, and I was just reaching my majority, with no knowledge of the world outside of the wilderness, and with no business experience, excepting in the fur trade. For the past five years I had had no opportunity to improve my mind by intercourse with refined society excepting during the short time I had passed in Chicago and Mackinaw, and while at the latter place, more than one-half of my time was devoted to hard labor. In my boyhood days I had no love for books or study and now that I felt the need of

improving my mind, I could find no opportunity to do
so. For the past year I had felt more than ever the
waste of my life and the mortification my ignorance
caused me.

Messrs. Kinzie and Wolcott strongly advised me to
remain in the only business for which I was fitted, and
to forego the pleasure of seeing my mother and sisters.
They advised me to remit my earnings and remain in
the Indian trade under some favorable arrangement with
the American Fur Company; or, if not with them, with
Mr. Choteau of St. Louis, who was ready to give me
employment at a good salary. To abandon a business
that had cost me five years to learn, under so many
privations and exposures, for some other uncertain
vocation, to fit me for which would consume valuable
time, seemed to them very inadvisable. "Demand,"
they said, "of the Fur Company a fair consideration for
your abilities, and if they refuse to give it, then you
have Mr. Choteau to fall back upon; and if both fail,
you are well-enough known to get credit for an outfit
and take chances on your own account."

I knew these gentlemen were among my best friends,
were disinterested in their advice, and knew better than
I did the estimation in which Messrs. Ramsay and Crooks
held me. Our coasting voyage gave me ample time to
ponder over my situation and determine the course to
pursue. I had a great desire to go home, if only for a
short visit. I had less than one hunded dollars due me,
had no respectable clothing; my best coat was the same
one provided for me when I left Montreal. It was not
threadbare, and would have looked quite well on me,
had the fashion been for buttons half way up the back

and sleeves short and tight. Five years before, it looked on me as though it was my father's; now it looked like a half-grown boy's. To have fitted myself out in a manner to be presentable to the society of Middletown would have cost all my accumulated funds. I was forced after due consideration to forego the pleasure of seeing those dear to me, and before reaching Mackinaw I had concluded to remain west—*where* to be decided when I saw Mr. Crooks. I felt certain of a good position in the employ of the Choteaus at St. Louis in case Mr. Crooks' terms were not satisfactory. When I reached Mackinaw I was a free man with more than ninety dollars to my credit on the books of the company.

Mr. Crooks desired me to again take charge of packing the furs, which I consented to do without any stipulation as to price, but on the condition that I should be at liberty to quit at any time by giving a few days' notice; this enabled me to send eighty dollars of my earnings to my mother. As I was at work earning wages I did not hesitate to get from the retail store, then in charge of John H. Kinzie, such goods and clothing as I desired.

In about a month a schooner arrived from Cleveland loaded with corn, tallow, and other provisions for the use of the Company. She was to take to Buffalo a cargo of furs, which were ready packed for shipment.

I had been negotiating for a re-engagement, but had declined the offer made by the managers and had demanded a larger salary, which had been refused. The morning after the arrival of the schooner I surprised Mr. Stewart by asking him to fill my place, as I had decided to take passage on the schooner for Buffalo, and requested him to fix my allowance, that I might settle my account at the store. I hoped that I should have enough left to take me east, and added that perhaps Mr. Astor would give me employment in the fur store in New York.

Mr. Stewart seemed much surprised, and said that he thought it was settled that I should remain in the employ of the Company. I replied "No, sir; I consider my services worth more than you and Mr. Crooks offer me; hence I intend to leave you." Before the departure of the schooner, however, they accepted my offer, and I engaged with the Company for another year. I shipped a portion of my goods to Chicago by a vessel bound there, and thus reduced the number of boats in the brigade to five.

Mr. Deschamps, having become old and worn by long continued service and the hardships to which he had been exposed, resigned his position as Superintendent of the Illinois River Trading Posts of the American Fur Company, and on his recommendation I was appointed to succeed him. I now determined to carry out a project which I had long urged upon Mr. Deschamps, but without success—that of unloading the boats upon their arrival at Chicago from Mackinaw, and scuttling them in the slough, to prevent their loss by prairie fires, until they were needed to reload with furs for the return voyage.

The goods and furs I proposed to transport to and from the Indian hunting grounds on pack horses. In this manner the long, tedious, and difficult passage through Mud Lake, into and down the Desplaines River, would be avoided, and the goods taken directly to the Indians at their hunting grounds, instead of having to be carried in packs on the backs of the men. During the year 1822, I had established a direct path or track from Iroquois post to Danville, and I now extended it south from Danville and north to Chicago, thus fully opening "Hubbard's Trail" from Chicago to a point about one hundred and fifty miles south of Danville. Along this "trail" I established trading posts forty to fifty miles apart. This "trail" became the regularly traveled route between Chicago and Danville and points beyond, and was designated on the old maps as "Hubbard's Trail." *

In the winter of 1833-34 the General Assembly ordered that a State road be located from Vincennes to Chicago, and that mile-stones be placed thereon, and from Danville to Chicago the Commissioners adopted my "trail" most of the way, because it was the most direct route and on the most favorable ground. Through constant use by horses, ponies, and men, the path became worn so deeply into the ground that when I last visited the vicinity of my old Iroquois post (now called Bunkum), in the fall of 1880, traces of it were still visible, and my grand nephew, a little lad of fourteen years, who accompanied me on the trip, jumped out of the carriage and ran some distance in the trail where I had walked fifty-eight years before.

*Note.—"Hubbard's Trail" ran through Cook, Will, Kankakee, Iroquois, and Vermilion Counties, passing the present towns of Blue Island, Homewood, Bloom, Crete, Grant, Momence, Beaverville, Iroquois, Hoopeston, and Myersville to Danville, and southwest through Vermilion and Champaign Counties to Bement in Piatt County; thence south through Moultrie and Shelby Counties to Blue Point in Effingham County. At Crete, a fence has been built around a portion of this "trail," to further preserve it as an old landmark and a relic of early roads and early times.—H. E. H.

1825.

The winter of 1825 I passed at my Iroquois post. The hunting had been unusually good, and large quantities of goods were sold and many fine furs collected.

In the spring, Mr. John Kinzie got out of goods at Chicago, and sent a Mr. Hall to me to request me to go to St. Louis by boat for a supply. Mr. Hall was to remain and manage my business during my absence. Neither Mr. Kinzie nor myself had a boat suitable for the journey, but he thought I could arrange for one. Mr. Hamlin, of Peoria, had a boat which was well adapted to the purpose, and I decided to send Vasseur and Portier to Peoria to engage the boat and prepare it for the journey, while I should go to Chicago, see Mr. Kinzie, and learn from him what goods were required.

The water was very high, and all the rivers and streams had overflowed their banks. Portier could not swim, and both men were afraid and refused to go. I assured them they would not need to swim, as they could head all the streams on the route; while, on the way to Chicago, I should be compelled to cross the streams, and probably to swim them. I further told them that if they refused to go, I should dock their wages and discharge them. In the morning, having thought the matter over and becoming ashamed of their refusal, they announced themselves as ready to start, and did so as soon as they had eaten their breakfasts. This was the first and only time they ever refused to obey my orders.

I thought I could go on horseback to the mouth of the Iroquois and there swim the Kankakee, and as two

Indians were bound for that point, I decided to accompany them. It had frozen during the night, and the morning was very cold. We progressed very pleasantly until we reached a small stream on the prairie which had overflowed its banks, and upon which a new covering of ice had formed during the night, leaving running water between the two coverings of ice. The upper ice was not strong enough for a man to walk on, but the Indians laid down and slid themselves across with little difficulty. I rode my horse to the stream, and reaching forward with my tomahawk broke the ice ahead of him, he walking on the under ice until he reached the middle of the stream, when his hind feet broke through, the girth gave away, and the saddle slipped off behind carrying me with it. I fell into the water and was carried by the current rapidly down the stream between the upper and lower coverings of ice. I made two attempts to gain my feet, but the current was so swift and the space so narrow I could not break through the ice.

I had about given up all hope, when my hand struck a willow bush near the bank and thus arrested my rapid progress. At the same time I stood up and bumping the ice with my head broke through. The Indians were much astonished to see me come up through the ice, and gave utterance to their surprise by a peculiar exclamation. I recovered my horse and saddle and returned to my trading house, with no worse result than wet clothing and a slightly bruised head.

I had just completed a small blackwalnut canoe, and with this, and my man Jombeau to assist me, I went to the dividing ridge, near where the city of Kankakee now stands. The canoe was small and would barely hold us both, but we paddled safely down the Iroquois, and the following day arrived at Kankakee; there we left the canoe and started for Chicago on foot. It was a warm, thawing day, and I could scarcely see on account of the mist. I had walked a long time and thought I was on my "trail" and near Blue Island, when I heard a gun, and soon after found an Indian, who had shot a muskrat. This I got from him, and it was all Jombeau and I had to eat that day and the following one.

The Indian asked where I was going, and when I told him to Chicago, he surprised us by saying that we were going the wrong way. We had become completely turned around, and were then only about two miles from "Yellow Head Point." We camped that night on the bank of a creek, near where Miller's stock-farm is now located. On the third day I reached Chicago, reported to Mr. Kinzie, and found that he had started two men in a canoe to meet me at Peoria with a list of the goods required.

The day following I started in another canoe with an old Frenchman for Peoria, and we got along without trouble until we reached Peoria Lake. The wind being fair, I made a small mast and hoisted a blanket for a sail; but the wind being quite strong, the canoe suddenly upset when about a half-mile from shore. My companion was terribly frightened, but I made him cling to the boat, and soon got him safely to land. We were three days in making the trip to Peoria. My men had arrived, and the boat was all prepared for the trip to St. Louis. They had become much alarmed about me, thinking I was drowned, and were greatly rejoiced at my arrival. The next day we started for St.

Louis, where we arrived in due season and without incident worthy of notice. I bought my goods, delivered them at Chicago, and returned as quickly as possible to my post at Iroquois.

We were in a state of semi-starvation this spring, being compelled to live almost entirely on corn. My men were busy splitting rails to fence in a patch of ground for a garden, in which I hoped to raise vegetables for the following winter's consumption. Meat was much desired, but hard to procure.

I had a large domestic cat that enjoyed the freedom of the house and store, and upon packing my winter's collection of furs for transportation to Chicago, I discovered that the cat had gnawed the ends of some of them, where meat had been left in skinning. I was very much vexed at the discovery. Looking up I saw the cat sitting in the store window, and taking my rifle, shot him. He fell inside, and crawled behind a bale of cloth, where he remained until I removed the goods, when I found and killed him. I took him out and gave him to the Indian cook, telling him that the skin would make him a nice tobacco pouch. Just before dinner time I went out again and asked the cook what he had done with the cat. He answered me by pointing to the kettle in which the corn soup was cooking for the men's dinner. I laughed, but said nothing.

When the men came in and smelled the savory stew they were greatly pleased at the thought of having meat for dinner. They were always in the habit of selecting the choicest bits of meat and sending them to me, and they did not forget me on this occasion; but I declined to eat, telling them I did not care for it, and that they could eat all of it. They ate it with great relish, and after they had finished their dinner. I asked them if they knew what they had eaten. They said "yes, wild-cat," and were greatly astonished when I told them they had devoured our old tom cat. One of them said it made no difference, it was good ; the other thought differ-ently, and tried hard to rid himself of what he had eaten by thrusting his finger down his throat, but without success : the old cat would not come up.

I had now been in the employ of the American Fur
Company for more than seven years, and for the two
years after the expiration of my original five years' con-
tract, I had received the very liberal salary of thirteen
hundred dollars per year. Being, however, dissatisfied
with that amount, I had determined to leave its employ, when the Company offered me an interest as a
special partner, which offer I gladly accepted. My labors were no lighter; in fact, the responsibility seemed
greater, and I worked harder than ever, realizing that
on my own efforts and success depended the amount
of compensation I should receive. My headquarters
for the winter were at Iroquois post, though I made
frequent excursions to other points, and was very often
in Chicago.

One cold day in March, 1827, I went to Beaver Creek
Lake for a hunt. This was a part of the great Kankakee
marsh, and geese, ducks, and swan were very abundant.
The fall previous I had hidden a canoe in the vicinity of
the lake and about thirteen miles from my trading house,

(143)

and this I found with little difficulty. I hunted until nearly dark, when, thinking it too late to return home, I camped for the night on a small island in the lake. There were no trees, but I made a fire with driftwood, and having cooked some game for my supper, lay down and soon fell asleep. Some time in the night I awoke in great pain, and found that my fire had nearly gone out. I managed to replenish it, but the pain continued, being most severe in my legs, and by morning it increased to such an extent that I could not reach my canoe. About ten o'clock an Indian came down the lake and I called him and told him of my condition, and with his assistance reached the canoe, and finally the main shore. I sent the Indian to Iroquois with orders for my men to come and bring with them a horse and harness. On their arrival I had the horse hitched to the canoe and myself placed therein, and started in this manner to ride home. I soon found that I could not stand the jarring of the canoe as it was drawn over the rough ground, and halted until some better means of travel could be devised. I sent back to Iroquois for two more men, which necessitated my camping for another night. On their arrival they constructed, with poles and blankets, a litter upon which they bore me safely and quite comfortably home.

I had a severe attack of inflammatory rheumatism, which confined me to the house for three or four weeks, and from which I did not fully recover for eighteen months. I doctored myself with poultices of elm and decoctions of various herbs.

About six weeks after my attack of rheumatism I prepared to abandon my trading house on the Iroquois

and remove to Chicago, but was compelled to wait for
a band of Indians who owed me for goods and who had
not yet returned from their winter hunting grounds.
While thus delayed two white men appeared with a pair
of horses and a wagon loaded with corn, cornmeal, and
whisky. Hearing that I was waiting for the Indians,
they decided to wait also and trade them whisky for furs,
blankets, or anything else of value which the Indians
might possess. I was unable to walk without crutches,
and scarcely able to leave my bunk. I knew that if the
Indians were allowed to have the whisky, trouble would
ensue, so I sent Noel Vasseur to their camp to ask one
of the men to come and see me. He soon came, and I
told him I did not like to have him sell whisky to the
Indians, and that he had no right to do so, as he had no
license from the Government to trade with Indians. He
replied that he had as much right to trade as I had, and
that he should do as he pleased. I warned him that the
Indians would become drunk, and would then rob, and
probably murder them, but he refused to listen to me,
and returned to his camp.

I immediately stationed men to watch for the coming
of the Indians, and was soon informed that Yellow Head
and his band were at hand. When they arrived, I had
a large kettle of corn soup and other food ready for them,
and as soon as they had eaten, I took them into my
council room, traded for their furs, collected what they
owed me, and after giving each one a gill of whisky,
dismissed them before the strangers had learned of their
arrival. The Indians soon discovered the camp of the
two men and commenced trading their blankets and the
goods they had just bought from me for whisky. I sent

word to the men to leave, and told them that as soon as the Indians got drunk they would rob them of all they had sold them, but they would not heed the message.

As I had anticipated, the Indians soon became drunk, and angry because they had nothing more to trade and could get no more to drink, and began to take back their blankets and goods. The white men became very much frightened, and came to me for assistance. I refused to interfere, but sent Vasseur and Jacques Jombeau to empty the remaining kegs of whisky, which they did. The Indians scooped up the whisky with their hands, and became more and more enraged, and finally assaulted Jombeau, and stabbed him in the back, though not severely. The Indians got back all they had sold, and the white men made their escape with the horses and wagon. The disturbance lasted all night.

The Indians came to my house and demanded more whisky, and were, of course, refused. They all laid down and fell asleep, except Yellow Head (a brother-in-law of Billy Caldwell), who came several times to me, coaxing and threatening me, but to no purpose. He finally said he would go to my store, break in and take as much as he wanted. I said, "Very well, go on," and he started for the storehouse. I got up from my bunk, took my rifle and thrust it through the paper which served for window glass, and as he reached the store, I "drew a bead on him," and called to him to go on and break in. He changed his mind and walked away.

I again laid down, and in a few minutes he returned very angry, and walking up to my bunk drew a knife and attempted to stab me; but I was too quick 'for him, seized his arm, and lame as I was, jumped up, took the knife away, and pushed him out of the door, where I found some squaws who had been attracted by the disturbance. Outside the door was a large mortar with a heavy iron-wood pestle, which I used for pounding corn. I gave the knife to a squaw, and leaned on one crutch against the mortar with my hand on the pestle. Yellow Head felt in his leggins for another knife, when I said to the squaw, "Give the old woman a knife." She did so, but Yellow Head, looking at the pestle upon which my hand rested, and doubtless remembering the sudden manner in which I had before disarmed him, deemed " discretion the better part of valor," and silently departed with the squaws.

The day following I started for Chicago, leaving one of my men, Dominick Bray by name, in charge of the place, and to make a garden and plant vegetables for the following winter's use. Two or three days after my arrival in Chicago, Bray appeared with the story that Yellow Head had returned for revenge. Bray was lying in his bunk, when Yellow Head and two other Indians entered the house and leveled their rifles at him. He jumped up and ran by them out of the door, pulling it shut just as they fired, and the bullets struck the door through which he had escaped. Bray ran into the woods, caught a horse, and left for Chicago. The Indians pillaged the house and store, taking everything that had been left. Other Indians warned me that Yellow Head intended to kill me should he ever meet me again, but before my return to the Iroquois, he was killed in a drunken fight, and thus I was saved from further trouble with him.

I had already located at Danville, where I intended in

the future to make my general headquarters, and a portion of the spring and summer of this year was spent at that place. Danville had become quite a settlement, and I had a number of pleasant acquaintances there. Mr. Kinzie having resigned his position as Indian trader at Chicago, I made application for the place, which, however, I did not receive.

I made my annual trip to Mackinaw, arriving there in the month of August, and before my return made a new arrangement with the Fur Company, by which I bought out its entire interests in Illinois. Business was very poor during the year 1827, and in the spring of 1828 I built a store at Danville, and permanently established my headquarters there.

WINNEBAGO SCARE. *

At the breaking out of the Winnebago war, early in July, 1827, Fort Dearborn was without military occupation.

Doctor Alexander Wolcott, Indian agent, had charge of the fort, living in the brick building, just within the north stockade, previously occupied by the commanding officers. The old officers' quarters, built of logs, on the west, and within the pickets, were occupied by Russell E. Heacock and one other American family, while a number of *voyageurs* with their families were living in the soldiers' quarters on the east side of the inclosure.

The annual payment of the Pottawatomie Indians occurred in September of the year 1828. A large body of them had assembled, according to custom, to receive their annuity. These left after the payment for their respective villages, except a portion of Big Foot's band.

* From statements by Mr. Hubbard in Chicago Historical Series, No. 10.

The night following the payment, there was a dance in the soldiers' barracks, during the progress of which a violent storm of wind and rain arose; and about midnight these quarters were struck by lightning and totally consumed, together with the storehouse and a portion of the guard-house.

The sleeping inmates of Mr. Kinzie's house, on the opposite bank of the river, were aroused by the cry of "*fire*," from Mrs. Helm, one of their number, who, from her window, had seen the flames. On hearing the alarm I, with Robert Kinzie, hastily arose, and, only partially dressed, ran to the river. To our dismay, we found the canoe, which was used for crossing the river, filled with water; it had been partially drawn up on the beach and became filled by the dashing of the waves. Not being able to turn it over, and having nothing with which to bail it out, we lost no time, but swam the stream. Entering by the north gate we saw at a glance the situation. The barracks and storehouse being wrapped in flames, we directed our energies to the saving of the guard-house, the east end of which was on fire. Mr. Kinzie, rolling himself in a wet blanket, got upon the roof. The men and women, about forty in number, formed a line to the river, and with buckets, tubs, and every available utensil, passed the water to him; this was kept up till daylight before the flames were subdued, Mr. Kinzie maintaining his dangerous position with great fortitude, though his hands, face, and portions of his body were severely burned. His father, mother, and sister, Mrs. Helm, had meanwhile freed the canoe from water, and crossing in it, fell into line with those carrying water.

Some of the Big Foot band of Indians were present at

the fire, but merely as spectators, and could not be prevailed upon to assist; they all left the next day for their homes. The strangeness of their behavior was the subject of discussion among us.

Six or eight days after this event, while at breakfast in Mr. Kinzie's house, we heard singing, faintly at first, but gradually growing louder as the singers approached. Mr. Kinzie recognized the leading voice as that of Bob Forsyth, and left the table for the piazza of the house, where we all followed. About where Wells street now crosses the river, in plain sight from where we stood, was a light birch-bark canoe, manned with thirteen men, rapidly approaching, the men keeping time with their paddles to one of the Canadian boat songs; it proved to be Governor Cass and his secretary, Robert Forsyth, and they landed and soon joined us From them we first learned of the breaking out of the Winnebago war, and the massacre on the Upper Mississippi. Governor Cass was at Green Bay by appointment, to hold a treaty with the Winnebagoes and Menomonee tribes, who, however, did not appear to meet him in council. News of hostilities reaching the Governor there, he immediately procured a light birch bark canoe, purposely made for speed, manned it with twelve men at the paddles and a steersman, and started up the river, making a portage into the Wisconsin, then down it and the Mississippi to Jefferson Barracks below St. Louis.

Here he persuaded the commanding officer to charter a steamer, and embarking troops on it, ascended the Mississippi in search of the hostile Indians, and to give aid to the troops at Fort Snelling. On reaching the mouth of the Illinois River, the Governor (with his men and canoe, having been brought so far on the steamer), here left it, and ascending that stream and the Desplaines, passed through Mud Lake into the South Branch of the Chicago River, thus reaching Chicago. This trip from Green Bay, was performed in about thirteen days; the Governor's party sleeping only five to seven hours, and averaging sixty to seventy miles travel each day. On the Wisconsin River they passed Winnebago encampments without molestation. They did not stop to parley, passing rapidly by, singing their boat songs; the Indians were so taken by surprise that before they recovered from their astonishment, the canoe was out of danger. Governor Cass remained at Chicago but a few hours, coasting Lake Michigan back to Green Bay. As soon as he left, the inhabitants of Chicago assembled for consultation. Big Foot was suspected of acting in concert with the Winnebagoes, as he was known to be friendly to them, and many of his band had intermarried with that tribe.

Shaub-e-nee was not here at the payment, his money having been drawn for him by his friend, Billy Caldwell. The evening before Governor Cass' visit, however, he was in Chicago, and then the guest of Caldwell. At my suggestion he and Caldwell were engaged to visit Big Foot's village (Geneva Lake), and get what information they could of the plans of the Winnebagoes, and also learn what action Big Foot's band intended taking. They left immediately, and on nearing Geneva Lake, arranged that Shaub-e-nee should enter the village alone, Caldwell remaining hidden.

Upon entering the village Shaub-e-nee was made a prisoner, and accused of being a friend of the Americans, and a spy. He affected great indignation at these charges, and said to Big Foot : " I was not at the payment, but was told by my braves that you desired us to join the Winnebagoes and make war on the Americans. I think the Winnebagoes have been foolish ; alone they cannot succeed. So I have come to council with you, hear what you have to say, when I will return to my people and report all you tell me ; if they shall then say we will join you, I will consent." After talking nearly all night they agreed to let him go, provided he was accompanied by one of their own number ; to this proposal Shaub-e-nee readily consented, though it placed him in a dangerous position. His friend Caldwell was waiting for him in the outskirts of the village and his presence must not be known, as it would endanger both of their lives. Shaub-e-nee was equal to the emergency. After leaving in company with one of Big Foot's braves, as the place of Caldwell's concealment was neared, he commenced complaining in a loud voice of being suspected and made a prisoner, and when quite near, said, " We must have no one with us in going to Chicago. Should we meet any one of your band or *any one else*, we must tell them to go away ; we must go by ourselves, and get to Chicago by noon to-morrow. Kinzie will give us something to eat and we can go on next day."

Caldwell heard and understood the meaning of this, and started alone by another route. Strategy was still to be used, as Shaub-e-nee desired to report ; so, on nearing Chicago he said to his companion, " If Kinzie sees you, he will ask why your band did not assist in putting out the fire. Maybe he has heard news of the war and is angry with Big Foot ; let us camp here, for our horses are very tired. This they did, and after a little the Big Foot brave suggested that Shaub-e-nee should go to the fort for food and information. This was what he wanted to do, and he lost no time in reporting the result of his expedition, and procuring food returned to his camp. Starting the next morning with his companion for his own village ; on reaching it he called a council of his Indians, who were addressed by Big Foot's emissary ; but they declined to take part with the Winnebagoes, advising Big Foot to remain neutral.

On receiving Shaub-e-nee's report, the inhabitants of Chicago were greatly excited. Fearing an attack, we assembled for consultation, when I suggested sending to the Wabash for assistance, and tendered my services as messenger. This was at first objected to, on the ground that a majority of the men at the fort were in my employ, and in case of an attack, no one could manage them or enforce their aid but myself. It was, however, decided that I should go, as I knew the route and all the settlers. An attack would probably not be made until Big Foot's embassador had returned with his report ; this would give at least two weeks' security, and in that time I could, if successful, make the trip and return. I started between four and five o'clock in the afternoon, reaching my trading house on the Iroquois River by midnight, where I changed my horse and went on ; it was a dark, rainy night. On reaching Sugar Creek I found the stream swollen out of its banks, and my horse refusing to cross, I was obliged to wait till daylight, when I discovered that a large tree had fallen across the trail, making the ford impassable. I swam the stream and went on, reaching my friend Mr. Spencer's house at noon, tired out.

Mr. Spencer started immediately to give the alarm, asking for volunteers to meet at Danville the next evening, with five days' rations. By the day following at the hour appointed, one hundred men were organized into a company, and appointing a Mr. Morgan, an old frontier fighter, as their captain, immediately started for Chicago, camping that night on the north fork of the Vermilion River. It rained continually, the trail was very muddy, and we were obliged to swim most of the streams and many of the large sloughs, but we still pushed on, reaching Fort Dearborn the seventh day after my departure, to the great joy of the waiting people.

We re-organized, and had a force of about one hundred and fifty men, Morgan commanding. At the end of thirty days, news came of the defeat of the Winnebagoes, and of their treaty with the commanding officer, who went from Jefferson Barracks, as before stated. Upon hearing this, Morgan disbanded his company, who returned to their homes, leaving Fort Dearborn in charge of the Indian agent as before.

NOTE.—Extract from a letter written by Mr. Hubbard to his sister Elizabeth, at Middletown, Conn.

CHICAGO, July 25, 1827.

You will undoubtedly hear through the medium of the newspapers of the hostilities lately commenced by the Winnebago Indians.

Governor Cass surprised us on the 21st by his arrival, and brought us the first intelligence of the depredations committed by that tribe. They commenced their hostilities at Prairie du Chien, by killing a family in open day. Afterward, a party of one hundred and fifty waylaid a boat descending the Mississippi, attacked it with great violence, and after a contest of two hours, withdrew. The boat's crew defended themselves bravely; their loss was two men killed and six wounded. The Indians lost fourteen men killed; the number of wounded was not ascertained.

I cannot close this communication without adding my
testimony regarding the character and services of that
noble Indian chief, Shaub-e-nee. From my first acquaintance with him, which began in the fall of 1818, to his
death, I was impressed with the nobleness of his character. Physically, he was as fine a specimen of a man
as I ever saw ; tall, well proportioned, strong, and active,
with a face expressing great strength of mind and good-
ness of heart. Had he been favored with the advantages of education, he might have commanded a high

---

The Governor was at the Prairie when the boat arrived, and counted two
hundred ball holes through her cargo box. All the forces from St. Louis
were immediately sent up to the Prairie to join those from the St. Peter's.
It is thought that the forces collected at the Prairie amount to seven thousand
men, part of whom are now doubtless in the enemy's country.

The war-club was in circulation here during the payment, with such
secrecy that not one of us knew anything of it until the Governor arrived,
when he was informed by a few friendly Indians

The principal Pottawatomie Indians were sent for, and a council held on
the 22d, when the Governor informed them of every particular. They
acknowledged that messages had been sent to them from the Winnebagoes,
but assured us of their friendship. We do not apprehend the least danger
from them, and those who live on the Illinois River are bringing their
families into our settlement for protection. The inhabitants of this place
are all assembled in the fort. We do not think that there is any danger,
but think it best to be on our guard.

The Governor left here yesterday for Green Bay. He will send a company of troops on here immediately to take possession of this fort. We
expect them in twenty days. I shall not leave here until I see my friends
out of all danger. You shall hear from me again shortly ; in the mean
time, do not be uneasy as to my safety. We have vigilant scouts out, and
get notice of any party of Indians before they could surprise us, although I
do not think there is the least danger of their making the attempt. Our
troops will give them enough to attend to in their own villages, and the war
can not last more than twenty or thirty days before they are all destroyed.
Again I beg you will not be uneasy ; I am in perfect safety.

position among the men of his day. He was remarkable
for his integrity, of a generous and forgiving nature,
always hospitable, and until his return from the West,
a strictly temperate man, not only himself abstaining
from all intoxicating liquors, but influencing his people
to do the same. He was ever a friend to the white
settlers, and should be held by them and their descend-
ants in greatful remembrance. He had an uncommonly
retentive memory, and a perfect knowledge of this
Western country. He would readily draw on the sand
or bed of ashes, quite a correct map of the whole district
from the lakes west to the Missouri River, giving general courses of rivers, designating towns and places of
notoriety, even though he had never seen them.

It has been reported that Shaub-e-nee said that Tecumseh was killed by Col. R. M. Johnson. This, I am convinced, is a mistake, for I have often conversed with
him on that subject, and he invariably said that balls
were striking all around them ; by one of them Tecumseh
was killed and fell by his side ; that no one could tell
who directed the fatal shot, unless it were the person
who fired it ; that person was claimed to be Johnson.

It ought to be a matter of regret and mortification to
us all that our Government so wronged this man, who
so often periled his own life to save those of the whites,
by withholding from him the title to the land granted
him under a solemn treaty, the Commissioners, representing our Government, having given him their pledge
that the land allotted him by the Pottawatomie Nation
should be guaranteed to him by our Government, and
he protected in its ownship. He never sold his right to
the land, but by force was driven from it. When he

returned from the West to take possession, he found that our Government, disregarding his rights, had sold it.*

The winter of 1830-31 was the most severe one I ever experienced in the Indian country, and was always remembered and spoken of by the early settlers as the "winter of the big snow." I was employed in gathering together hogs to drive to Chicago to kill and sell to the settlers and soldiers at Fort Dearborn, a business in which I was then regularly engaged. I also had a store at Danville stocked with goods suitable for trade with the white settlers of that section of country.

On the seventh of November, 1830, I started out to gather up my hogs, which were in small droves at different points on the road. The snow was then about seven inches deep, and it continued to fall for four or five days. I had men to help me, and wagons containing corn for

* I have no information as to Mr. Hubbard's life during the years 1828-29 further than that he was engaged in a general business at Danville, and still retained his trading post at Iroquois. During these years he dealt quite extensively in farm produce, and had contracts for furnishing beef and pork to the troops stationed at Fort Dearborn. He continued his annual visits to Mackinaw, and during his life as a fur trader, made twenty-six trips to and from that island, coasting Lake Michigan in an open row-boat. In 1828 he went on horseback and alone to Detroit without seeing any indications of a white settlement until he reached Ypsilanti, at which place were a few log houses. In the winter of 1829 he killed a large number of hogs, and not having received the barrels, which were to arrive by vessel, he piled the pork up on the river bank, near where Rush street now is, and kept it in that manner until the arrival of barrels in the spring. This was the beginning of the packing industry in Chicago. During the summer of 1830 he, for the first time, returned to the East and visited his mother and family at Middletown, Conn. His sisters Mary (afterwards Mrs. Dr. Clark) and Abby (afterwards Mrs. A. L. Castleman) returned with him to his home in Danville, where they continued to reside until they were married.—H. E. H.

the hogs, in which were also our blankets and utensils. When we left Beaver Creek marsh the weather had changed, and the day was rainy and misty. At dark we had reached the Kankakee and camped in a little hollow, having left the hogs a mile or so back. It rained hard a portion of the night, and then the wind changed and it began freezing. The water gradually worked under the blanket and buffalo robe in which I had wrapped myself, and on attempting to rise I found myself frozen fast to the ground, and had much difficulty in freeing myself.

In the morning we gathered the hogs and drove them to the hollow in which we had camped, where we left them with our horses and started to find Billy Caldwell, who I knew was camped somewhere near Yellow Head Point, which was about six miles from Kankakee. Following up the creek we found him without difficulty, and were hospitably received by both Caldwell and his wife. Mrs. Caldwell made us some tea, and never in my life did I drink such quantities of anything as I did of that.

We remained at Caldwell's a day and night, when we again started the hogs for Chicago, where we arrived in about thirty days. The snow was about two feet deep on a level and four or five feet in the drifts. I killed and delivered my pork, and with empty wagons started on my return to Iroquois. Much of the way we were compelled to cut a passage through the snow and ice, and were ten days in making the trip. We had lost some of the hogs, and on our return we found one poor brute under the snow, where he had managed to subsist upon the roots of grass. Of course we killed him to save him from the slow torture of starvation.

It was a bitter cold night when we arrived at the Kankakee River, which we found very high and full of floating ice, with no possibility of fording it. My wagon was one of those heavy, large-box vehicles called a "Pennsylvania wagon," the box of which we chinked with snow, over which we poured water, which soon froze and made it water tight. Into this we put our harness, blankets, and utensils, and using it for a boat passed safely over, the horses being made to swim after. From this point we progressed at the rate of five to eight miles a day, and camped at Beaver Creek the evening of the second day thereafter. It had again rained, and all the channels and streams were high, and Beaver Creek had overflowed its banks, so I determined to go from there to Iroquois alone and send a man back with a horse and canoe to help get the others across. I cut a dry tree for a raft and got onto it, when an Indian, who was one of the party, said he wanted to cross also. I told him it was impossible; that the tree would only hold one, and he must wait for the canoe which I would send. We had a long rope which he proposed to tie to the log, and so draw it back after I had crossed, and to this I foolishly assented. When I had reached the middle of the stream I found I could advance no further, and on looking back found the Indian was holding the rope too tight, and I called to him to let go. On his doing so, and the log being released, it turned suddenly over and threw me into the stream. I swam ashore, and when I landed my clothes were frozen stiff, and I was near perishing with the cold.

My favorite horse, "Croppy," who had watched my departure and progress, was much excited, and neighed, pawed the ground, and whinnied so that I decided to allow him to come across. I called to Vasseur and told him to get my dry neips and moccasins from my saddle-bags, place them on the horse's head under the headstall, and let him loose. I called to Croppy and he swam across to me.

The bank was precipitous, and I had great difficulty in getting him up, he having drifted down below the ford, but I finally succeeded. I was sheeted with ice, but by alternately riding and running, made the sixteen miles to my house in good time, and sent Portier back with a horse and canoe loaded with provisions for the men and corn for the horses.

The canoe was used as a sleigh, and in it Portier rode and drove. He reached the men late at night and with his feet badly frozen. The day following all crossed the stream and arrived at home. We had been twenty days traveling seventy-five miles.

I had a small outfit up the Kankakee River, about six or eight miles from where "Hubbard's Trail" crossed the Kankakee, where two men were located. A day or so before the occurence above narrated, one of these men started for my trading house, and in attempting to cross Beaver Creek, at or near the place where I crossed, was drowned. Not returning as soon as he was expected, his companion sent an Indian to notify me of his absence, and search was made for him, but nothing could be seen or heard of him. The following spring an Indian going up Beaver Creek in a canoe, found his skeleton lodged in the branches of a fallen tree, about ten miles below the crossing, to which place it had been carried by the current.

Mr. Hubbard's autobiography ends here. What further information in regard to his life, until it became a part of the history of Chicago, I have been able to obtain, is from sources other than his own recital. For many years he kept a diary and noted the particulars of his everyday life. This was loaned to Colonel McRoberts, and though I have made considerable effort, I have been unable to recover it.

In the spring of 1831 he was married to Miss Elenora Berry, of Urbana, Ohio, and on his wedding trip to Louisville, Ky., was the hero of the following incident: Dr. Fithian, then and now a resident of Danville, furnishes the facts in a letter written to Mr. Hubbard in May, 1884. Dr. Fithian says:

"I write you all I remember relative to your saving the life of the child of Mr. Linton, then a merchant of Terre Haute, Indiana.

"You will remember that we both, with our wives, who were sisters, took passage at Perrysville, Indiana, early in the spring on the steamboat *Prairie Queen* for Cincinnati, and at Terre Haute, Indiana, Mr. Linton and his family came on board bound for the same place. I can not now recollect dates (being over seventy-five years of age), but I can recollect vividly the circumstance of the child falling overboard while passing up the Ohio River, which was very high and filled with floating ice. We were sitting out on the guard with other passengers, when Mr Linton's little boy slipped overboard and went feet foremost into the water. He was dressed in a blouse waist, which became filled with air and acted as a buoy, preventing him from sinking; and at this moment of writing it seems to me I can almost hear Mr. Linton, as

11

his child dropped into the water from the little steamboat, cry out, "Oh! my God, what shall I do? I cannot swim"; and I recollect that instant of time so vividly, that, blind as I am now, I see you throw off your coat and boots, plunge into the raging river, and swim for the drowning child; and I can recollect very distinctly the moment when we saw that you had reached the child, had turned upon your back and was floating in the water, and in that position held the child elevated in your hands. At this moment was the time for thought and action with those on the boat. You will recollect that there was no yawl nor small craft of any kind attached to the little steamer, and the excitement increased as this fact became known. All realized that something must be done speedily or both you and the child would be lost. Captain Cummings suggested, as the only thing that could be done, turning the steamer down stream and overtaking you, running out the walking-plank on the side, securing the end remaining on the boat as best could be done, so that some one could go out on the plank and assist in getting you and the child on board. This course was adopted successfully. While the steamer was being turned in the stream, and the walking plank being adjusted and made secure, blankets were taken to the engine-room and thoroughly heated, and all the mustard necessary got ready.

"When we had succeeded in getting you both on board again, the child was immediately pronounced dead by nearly everyone who was permitted to see him, but being taken to the engine-room at once and manipulated industriously, he ejected a considerable quantity of water, and by close watching, stimulating, and application of heat,

the circulation was soon discernible, and within an hour
he began to breathe pretty freely. During all this time
your wife and mine knew nothing of what had happened,
having been confined in the ladies' cabin by the captain,
who had filled up the stairs leading from it with trunks,
so that they could not get down.

"As a further proof that you are regarded as having
saved the child's life, I mention that Mr. Linton, father
of the child, as an evidence of his gratitude to you, insisted upon changing, and did actually change, the little
boy's name to that of Gurdon S. Hubbard Linton."

Dr. Fithian's letter was written in reply to one from
Mr. Hubbard, called out by the fact that some persons
had doubted that he could support himself and a child by
floating on his back in a swift current amid floating ice.

During Mr. Hubbard's residence in Danville he devoted
his time mainly to the conduct of his store at that place.
The fur trade had been nearly abandoned, and but few
Indians remained on this side of the Mississippi. A
small band of Kickapoos and a few Pottawatomies were
all that were left on the eastern side of the State. With
these Mr. Hubbard retained his friendship, and two boys,
aged ten and twelve respectively, were taken into his
family to be taught by his sisters. They remained with
him several months, and proved to be very intelligent,
conscientious and affectionate.

At the head of the band of Kickapoos was a chief
called the Prophet, whose name, however, was Ka-ne-
kuck. He was a Christian, and very much devoted to
the welfare of his tribe, and through his influence the
band then remaining had become strictly temperate, and
many of them were professing Christians.

The following is a translation, made by Mr. Hubbard, of a sermon preached by Ka-ne-kuck, and is copied from the *Illinois Monthly Magazine:*

A KICKAPOO SERMON.

"This discourse of Ka-ne-kuck, an Indian chief of the Kickapoo tribe of Indians, was delivered at Danville, Illinois, July 17, 1831. The citizens of the town and its vicinity had assembled at a Baptist meeting, and this Indian, who with a part of his tribe was encamped in the neighborhood, and in the habit of preaching to his tribe, was informed that the white people wished to hear his discourse. He requested G. S. Hubbard, Esq., who understands the language, to interpret for him. The congregation went to the Indian encampment early in the day, and before preaching commenced in the town. The chief caused mats to be spread upon the ground for his white audience to sit upon. His Indian brethren were also seated near him ; he then commenced and addressed the assembly for almost an hour. Mr. Hubbard repeated with great distinctness and perspicuity, each sentence, as spoken by the chief, and which was accurately written down at the time by Solomon Banta, Esq. It is proper to remark, that Ka ne-kuck was at one time given to intemperance. About four years since, he reformed, and is now esteemed a correct, pious, and excellent man. He has acquired an astonishing influence over his red brethren, and has induced all of his particular tribe, supposed to be near two hundred, and about one hundred Potawatomies who have been inveterate drunkards, to abstain entirely from the use of ardent spirits. It is proper further to remark that

Ka-ne-kuck is called a prophet among the Indians, but is not the *old prophet*, brother to Tecumseh, who is known to be not less odious among the Indians than among the whites, nor is he related to him. Ka-ne-kuck appears to be about forty years of age; is over the ordinary size; and, although an untutored savage, has much in his manner and personal appearance to make him interesting. He is much attached to the whites, and has had his son at school, with a view to give him an education.

The speech now presented for publication derives much of its interest from the fact that it is the discourse of an uneducated man of the forest, who is believed to have done more in his sphere of action in the cause of temperance, than any other man has effected, armed with all the power which is conferred by learning and talent. The fact of the influence attributed to Ka-ne-kuck upon this subject, is fully attested by gentlemen who are intimately acquainted with these Indians, and have known them for many years, and is, therefore, entitled to the fullest confidence.

My Friends : Where are your thoughts to-day? Where were they yesterday? Were they fixed upon doing good? or were you drunk, tattling, or did anger rest in your hearts? If you have done any of these things, your Great Father in heaven knows it. His eye is upon you. He always sees you, and will always see you. He knows all your deeds. He has knowledge of the smallest transactions of your lives. Would you not be ashamed if your friends knew all your bad thoughts and actions? and are you not ashamed that your Great Father knows them, and that He marks them nicely? You would be ashamed of appearing here to-day with bloated faces and swelled eyes, occasioned by drunkenness. You will one day have to go down into the earth; what will you do then, if you have not followed your Great Father's advice, and kept His commandments? He has given us a small path; it is hard to be followed; He tells you it leads to happiness.

Some of you are discouraged from following this path, because it is difficult to find. You take the broad road that leads to misery. But you ought not to be discouraged; mind the book he has given for your instruction; attend to its commands, and obey them, and each step you take in this narrow path will be easier; the way will become smoother, and at the end great will be the reward. The broad road some of you choose, is full of wide and deep pits; those who follow it are liable to fall into those pits; they are filled with fire for the punishment of all wicked and ill men. All professed drunkards, tattlers, liars, and meddling bodies are in the broad way; they can never be received into good places; their deeds are dark; they never see light. Parents who do not teach their children the difference between good and evil, are in the bad road. Your Great Father once came into this world. He came but once, and staid but a short time; that is the reason the good path is so narrow.

The bad spirit is with you always; he is abroad upon the face of the earth, and traveling in all places; that is the reason why the way that leads to misery is so broad.

The Great Father gave you a good book filled with commands. If you follow the commands, you will go into a good place and be happy forever; but if you do not keep them, you will go into a place prepared for the wicked, and suffer endless days and nights of grief. Some of you think you can indulge in drink once, and then you resolve to follow the good commands. But are you sure, if you indulge once, you can refrain for the time to come?

Your Great Father sees all you do. Is it not almost certain that you will always be repeating bad deeds? You are all sinners; you can not be too much on your guard, lest you tread out of the right way into the broad road. His eye notices the smallest thing, and if you wish to be good, your thoughts must be on your Great Father always; He takes pleasure when he sees your thoughts are placed on Him. If you would all be good you would all travel one road, and there would be but one road, and your Great Father would be with you always. But this can not be; every one knows when he is doing good, and if he is always conscious of doing good, he will be received by the Great Father; therefore guard with care every step you take in your life. One step a day in the narrow road is better than fifteen steps a day in the road to ruin. The door of heaven is always open, and the Great Father is glad to receive His children; those who go there will have happiness without end—will see their Great Father, and live with Him, and never be without Him. If young folks would but hold as fast to the good book as old and crippled people do to their canes which support them, there would be no danger of disobeying its commands. Every day you obey Him the better it is for you, and the easier it is for you to follow the good path. You must always notice well where you step, for fear you may be tempted out of the right path. When you see assemblies of amusement, you ought to reflect that to enter those may lead you to do things contrary to your Great Father's will.

He has said He will help those who keep His commands; therefore, you must always notice your hearts; the heart is the fountain from which good or evil thoughts flow. You are not mere forms, incapable of knowledge, but the Great Father has so made you that you may get a knowledge within yourselves, and if you are good, you will always see Him; if you place your thoughts upon Him, He will never desert you; but they who do not place their thoughts upon Him will be deserted—they travel the broad road and fall into the pit; their lot is fixed—they can not touch, nor see good; they will be in endless darkness—they never can see their friends, their father, mother, brothers, or sisters; their friends will be always grieving for them—they go where none but fools go, such as drunkards, liars, tattlers, and those who treat old people ill; they never can taste good; nothing can mitigate their sorrow and the torment they suffer. What will become of those wicked men who slight the commands of their Great Father? He gave them a book containing instructions to enlighten them. Who made that book? The Great Father made it for their good; long ago he made it, that their and our hearts might be strong, and that by reading it you might see Him, that you might not lose yourselves; a long time ago He gave this to instruct His children, and can there yet be such fools as will not receive instruction from so good a Father?

The Great Father, by His Son, once came upon earth; many people saw Him; He came in the form of a man, and staid a short time on the earth with His children. He is to come once more, when the wicked will not be noticed by Him—a great many hundreds will be lost; then we will see who has obeyed His book, and kept His commands. If your hearts are fixed on your Great Father, He will be pleased; but if they are not, where will you be going? No supplication will then avail—you will have no opportunity to kneel to Him—the time is past, He will not allow it; your friends can not intercede, fear will overwhelm you, you will wish to make new resolutions to obey Him, but you can not, you will go to the burning pits.

Your Great Father has implanted in your hearts a knowledge of good and evil, and shown you how to obey Him; if you do not, the time will come when you will not see yourselves as you are— you will be lost in darkness—all your former wickedness will prey upon you. Friends, you all see my brothers (pointing to his Indian brethren), they do not drink strong liquors as they once did; they do not shake their fists at you and abuse you; they do not quarrel with each other. Their thoughts are upon their Great Father; they are not liars and tattlers, fond of ridiculing old folks and children, as they used to be; their conduct toward their children is different. For a long time they have refrained from the bad practices of stealing and drunkenness; their Great Father will receive them into His own place, where they will be happy; they will never hunger nor thirst; they will see their children around them; their Great Father loves their hearts, for they are strong. Why, then, should they not love Him? He tells them He loves them; He gives them an opportunity to know Him; the Great Father has instilled into them a knowledge of good and evil by His works; He has not instructed them by books. He loves His children both red and white. I have done."

On the breaking out of the Black Hawk war in 1832, Mr. Hubbard induced Colonel Moore, who commanded the Vermilion County militia, to call out his regiment and march at once to the scene of hostilities, himself furnishing provisions, ammunition, and transportation wagons.

Three days after the news of the commencement of hostilities was received they departed, and on reaching Joliet they built a stockade fort, which they garrisoned with one company, and proceeded to East Du Page, where a similar defense was constructed and garrisoned, and the remainder of the regiment marched to Starved Rock, where they were disbanded. Mr. Hubbard then joined a company of scouts for sixty days, and served in that capacity until the company was disbanded. While connected with Colonel Moore's regiment he commanded the advance, and found and buried the body of Rev. Adam Payne, who had been murdered by the Indians.

Mr. Hubbard represented Vermilion County in the eighth General Assembly, which convened December 3, 1832, and adjourned March 2, 1833. During this session he introduced a bill for the construction of the Illinois & Michigan Canal, which passed the house, but was defeated in the senate. He then substituted a bill for a railroad, which was also defeated in the senate by the casting vote of the presiding officer. He attended every session of the Legislature thereafter to urge the passage of a canal bill, until the bill was finally passed in 1835 36.

Mr. Hubbard, Wm. F. Thornton, and Wm. B. Archer were appointed by Governor Duncan the first board of Canal Commissioners, in 1835. They served until 1841, when their successors were elected by the Legislature under a new law which deprived the Governor of the appointive power.

On July 4, 1836, the commencement of the canal was celebrated, and Mr. Hubbard dug the first spadeful of earth.

In 1834 he moved from Danville to Chicago and took

up his permanent residence there. He erected, at the corner of La Salle and South Water streets, the first large brick building in Chicago, which was called by the inhabitants "Hubbard's Folly," because of its size and the permanent manner of its construction.

By act of the Legislature, February 11, 1835, the "Town of Chicago" was incorporated, with Gurdon S. Hubbard, John H. Kinzie, Ebenezer Goodrich, John K. Boyer, and John S. C. Hogan as its first trustees. It comprised all the territory covered by sections 9 and 16, north and south fractional section 10, and fractional section 15, all in town 39 north, range 14 east of the third principal meridian; "provided that the authority of the Board of Trustees of the said town of Chicago shall not extend over the south fractional section 10 until the same shall cease to be occupied by the United States."*

He was also a director of the Chicago branch of the State Bank of Illinois. He was one of the incorporators of the Chicago Hydraulic Company, which built its works at the foot of Lake street, and supplied the south and a part of the west side with water until its franchises were purchased by the city in 1852. In 1848 he was one of the organizers of the Chicago Board of Trade.

In 1836 he sold out his mercantile business and built a warehouse fronting on Kinzie street and the river, and organized the firm of Hubbard & Co.—Henry G. Hubbard and Elijah K. Hubbard being his partners.

This firm embarked largely in the forwarding and commission business, and became interested in a great

*From report of Commissioner of Public Works, Dec. 31, 1880.

number of vessels and steamers forming the "Eagle Line," between Buffalo and the upper lakes. In this year he wrote for the Ætna Insurance Company the first policy ever issued in Chicago, and continued as agent of that and other companies until 1868. The previous year he had gone more extensively into the packing business, and had cut up and packed thirty-five hundred hogs. This business he continued, and was for many years known as the largest packer in the West. In 1868 his large packing house was destroyed by fire, and he then abandoned the business.

In later years, in connection with A. T. Spencer, he established a line of steamers to Lake Superior, among which were the *Superior* and *Lady Elgin*. The *Superior* was lost on the rocks in Lake Superior, and the loss of the *Lady Elgin* is familiar history. After the loss of his packing house he engaged in the direct importation of tea from China, and organized a company for that purpose. The great fire of October 9, 1871, destroyed his business, burned his property, and crippled him financially, and from that time he retired from active business life.

The Hon. Grant Goodrich, in a memorial read before the Chicago Historical Society, says of him :

" There are few of the numerous veins of commerce and wealth-producing industries that draw to this pulsating heart of the great West that boundless agricultural and mineral wealth, which through iron arteries and water craft is distributed to half a world, that have not felt the inspiration of his genius, and been quickened by his enterprise and energy. The assertion that in the progress of events, one who has reached the ordinary limit of human life in this age has lived longer than the oldest antediluvian, is surely verified in the life of Mr. Hubbard. What marvelous transformation he witnessed. When he reached Mackinaw at scarce sixteen years of age, save in the vicinity of Detroit, Michigan, the northern part of Indiana and Illinois, all Wisconsin and the limitless West which lies beyond—except here and there a trading post—was an unbroken wilderness, pathless, except by lakes and rivers and the narrow trail of the Indian and trapper. Sixty-eight years have passed, and what a change ! It challenges all historic parallel. Before the march of civilization the wild Indian has disappeared, or been driven toward the setting sun ; the dark forests and prairie, garden fields where he roved in the pride of undisputed dominion, have been transformed into harvest fields, dotted with villages and cities, some of them crowded with hundreds of thousands of inhabitants, where the hum of varied industry is never silent, and the smoke of forges and factories darkens the sky.

"The canoe and open boat have given place to thousand-ton vessels, and steamers of twice that burden. The narrow trails over which the Indian trotted his pony, are traversed or crossed by roads of iron, on which iron horses rush along with the speed of the wind. The amazing change may be more strikingly realized when we remember that while within the present limits of Cook County, there were then only three dwellings of white men outside of the garrison inclosure, there now dwell more than eight hundred thousand people, and that the seat of political power in this great Nation has been transferred to the valley of the Mississippi ; that it has made it possible to scale the heights of the Rocky

Mountains with railroads, and bring the Atlantic and Pacific Oceans into near neighborhood, and bind the East and West together with bands of steel.

"History has made immortal the names and achievements of men who have subdued, or founded, states and empires by force and sanguinary war. Do not these early pioneers, who, armed with the arts of peace, bravely met the dangers and endured the toils necessary to subjugate the great western wilderness to the abodes of peace and blessings of education, enlightened freedom, and the elevating appliances of civilization, merit equal admiration and gratitude as lasting?

"Those who believe that in the world's coming history its crowned heroes and benefactors are to be those who win the bloodless victories of peace, and by acts of self-sacrifice and beneficence scatter widest the blessings of Christian civilization, will hold these men, and Gurdon S. Hubbard as a prince among them, in highest honor and esteem."

We turn now to the personal, social, and private life of Mr Hubbard. While perfection can be claimed for no man, he appears to have borne himself, in all the duties pertaining to these relations, in a manner deserving commendation and respect. He was married in 1831 to Miss Elenora Berry, of Ohio, who died in Chicago in 1838, six days after the birth of their son. In 1843 he was married to Miss Mary Ann Hubbard, of Chicago, who, through the years of his helpless blindness, attended upon his every want with the constant devotion of a true and loving wife.

In the discharge of his filial and fraternal obligations he set an example of highest admiration. As before stated, during his service with the Fur Company he gave eighty dollars a year of his wages of one hundred and twenty dollars, toward the maintenance of his mother and dependent sisters. Afterwards, when his income was increased, enlarged their allowance, and until his mother died was their main support, which was continued to his sisters down to his death. To provide against all contingencies, he executed a deed of trust, some twenty years ago, and also by his last will, provided for their support during life. Socially, he was genial, sympathetic, and affable. His remarkable life and experiences made him interesting and instructive. He was thoughtfully careful of the feelings, and charitable to the faults, of others. Firm in his convictions and principles, but never intolerant, he was always the dignified and courteous gentleman. As a neighbor he was kind, and as a friend faithful and confiding. His heart overflowed with sympathy for the poor and unfortunate, and his hand was always open for their relief. As a husband he was carefully tender, loving and true : as a parent affectionate, generous, and indulgent. As a citizen he was patriotic and earnest in the promotion of what he believed for the best interests of his country. These worthy traits of character are the more remarkable, when we remember that his youth and early manhood were spent away from parental restraints, and amidst scenes of temptation and influences so adverse to strict morals and Christian obligations. But the religious principles imbibed from his mother's lips and the schools of those early days, seemed to have exercised a controlling influence over him.

I think it due him I should give the following extracts

from letters of Ramsey Crooks, the active head of the American Fur Company, and one from Mr. Stewart, the Secretary :

Under date of April, 1820, Mr. Crooks says : "Gurdon has thus far behaved himself in an exemplary manner for one of his age."

In a letter of March, 1826, urging Mrs. Hubbard to visit her son, he says : "You will see him at his daily duties, and you will see what will gladden the heart of a Christian mother, how faithfully he performs his daily duties, how much he is loved and respected by his employers and friends."

August 3, 1821, Mr. Stewart writes her: "He spends his winters with an old gentleman of finished education and correct gentlemanly manners. His account of your son is as flattering as a fond mother could wish. * * He is strictly sober, and, I believe, a great economist. I feel that I state the truth when I tell you I think him exempt from the vices which too frequently attend youth of his age." These commendations speak for themselves. In his church associations he was an Episcopalian. He was one of those who organized St. James Episcopal Church, the first of that denomination existing in Chicago, and of which he subsequently became a communicant.

In January, 1883, he was taken with chills, and in the following May lost the sight of his left eye, from which time he suffered from blood poisoning and frequent abscesses, and from almost constant pains in his eyes and neck. In the succeeding April, the eye was removed, and, though eighty-two years old, without anesthetics of any kind, or any one to hold his hands; the steady nerve and self control that so distinguished him in his earlier years, enabled him simply to lie down and have his eye cut out.   In July, 1885, the sight of his remaining eye was extinguished, leaving him in the horrors of total darkness ; about one year ago, his remaining eye was also removed, greatly relieving him from torturing pains.

Such a calamity and rayless darkness can neither be imagined nor described.   But in him, the fruits of the discipline of suffering were beautifully exhibited in uncomplaining submission to the Divine will, and patient endurance of his affliction, through all the long night of his blindness ; in his grateful sense of the sympathy of friends, and tender thankfulness for the helpful care and attentions of his loved ones.   It was manifest that, while material things were excluded from his sight, his nature was more fully conformed and assimilated to that of his Divine Redeemer, by the contemplation of the spiritual and unseen ; and on the 14th day of September, 1886, at the age of eighty-four years, he fell peacefully to sleep with the full assurance he would awaken into supernal light, with restored and immortal vision."

MEMORIAL.

UNDERWRITERS' MEMORIAL.

CHICAGO, October 19, 1886.

MRS. GURDON S. HUBBARD—*Dear Madame:* I hand you herewith a copy of minute adopted by the Chicago Fire Underwriters' Association, at a meeting held September 27, last, expressive of the appreciation in which the life and services of Mr. Hubbard are held by its members.

It is hardly necessary for me to assure you that the minute expresses a genuine feeling of sorrow that a long and useful life has come to an end. Such sorrow, however, is tempered by the reflection that he, whose energy and integrity have been among the motives the result of which has been the mighty city among whose citizens we are proud to be reckoned, has gone to the reward that awaits the just in the "City of our God."

I am, your obedient servant,

R. N. TRIMINGHAM, *Secretary.*

At a special meeting of the Chicago Fire Underwriters' Association, held September 27, 1886, the following minute was unanimously adopted:

Gurdon S. Hubbard, the oldest resident of Chicago, and the first of its underwriters, was born at Windsor, Vermont, August 22, 1802, and died September 14, 1886. It is eminently proper that the representatives of the underwriting interests of to-day should meet to commemorate in some fitting words his life and death.

Mr. Hubbard came to Chicago as a fur trader nearly seventy years ago. He found a fort and an Indian trading post. Before he died the trading post had grown to be the fourth city in the United States. In his life he saw the Indian give place to the settler, the fort succeeded by the village, the village by the town, and the town by a great city. He saw the wilderness change into the wealth-producing farms and the comfortable homes of millions of people, and the fur barter of a few Indians at the mouth of the Chicago River changed into the mighty commerce of a city of six hundred thousand inhabitants. Mr. Hubbard did not sit supinely and

(180)

watch this growth content to reap the harvest without being himself an active laborer in the field. He not only shared in the commercial enterprises that made the city what it is, but he was the originator and the pioneer in many of the most important of them. He was one of the first and the most active as a merchant in developing trade with the surrounding country; he fostered the transportation interests of the lakes and was himself at one time a large shipowner; he was one of the first, if not the first, to establish the industry, now so important, of packing cattle and hogs, and he was the first representative of that great interest which goes hand in hand with commerce and manufacture, protecting and sustaining them; the interest of which we assembled here are the present representatives.

Mr. Hubbard wrote the first insurance policy ever written in Chicago, fifty years ago, for the Ætna Insurance Company, of Hartford. He continued to represent the Ætna and other insurance companies many years after this, at first by himself, and later in partnership with the late Charles H. Hunt, and his name is closely associated with both the fire and the marine insurance transactions of those early days. Throughout his entire career as merchant, manufacturer, and underwriter, Mr. Hubbard maintained a course marked by so much integrity, that we of a later generation may well record as we do in these few words our appreciation of his life and our respect for his character. Therefore,

Be it Resolved, That in the death of Mr. Hubbard we feel not only the loss of a true friend, a useful and honorable citizen, a Christian gentleman, but of the father of our profession in this city.

Resolved, That the association do extend our heartfelt sympathies to the family, and as they mourn the loss of a kind husband and father, we also mourn the loss of a true man, one whose many years of upright and faithful leadership commanded not only our respect and confidence, but our love and admiration, one whose entire life-record is a golden legacy beyond all price.

Resolved, That this minute be spread on our records, and a copy be forwarded to the family of the deceased.

S. M. MOORE,
GEO. C. CLARKE,
EDWARD M. TEALL,
WM. E. RICE,
HENRY H. BROWN,
Committee.

CHARLES W. DREW, *President.*
R. N. TRIMINGHAM, *Secretary.*

TRIBUTE OF REV. G. S. F. SAVAGE, D. D.

In the recent death of Mr. Gurdon S. Hubbard, at the ripe age of eighty-four years, there passed away not only the oldest settler of Chicago, but a man who has filled a large and honorable place from the beginning in her wonderful history. Well-merited tributes have been paid by the public press to his character and achievements as a citizen, a business man, and a friend. But there is one aspect of his character, especially developed in the closing years of his eventful life, which deserves a more distinct recognition, viz.: his strong Christian faith and trust in the Lord Jesus Christ as his personal Savior; his love of the Bible as the inspired Word of his heavenly Father, and his uncomplaining submission to God's will under the severe discipline of his providence.

In middle life he became a professed Christian—a member of the Protestant Episcopal church, whose services he greatly prized. He was one of the founders and officers of the first Episcopal church established in Chicago—the St. James—and a liberal supporter of the same. And it was with much pain and large sacrifice to himself that he left her communion, when dissatisfied with what he believed to be the unscriptural and ritualistic doctrines and practices which had crept into the church of his love. Yet, as a matter of principle, when the time came for action, he did not hesitate to leave it, and join the then small and despised Reformed Episcopal church, cheerfully giving his influence, counsel, and pecuniary aid to this new and struggling organization.

During all those years of intensely active business life he maintained a Christian character above reproach. But it was in the closing years of his life, when the infirmities of age, and disease, and blindness laid him aside from his accustomed activities, that there was such a marked development of Christian character, and of a rich Christian experience, as attracted the special attention of friends, and became worthy of special note. Amid all the weaknesses, total blindness, and sufferings of the last two years of his life he did not lose his interest in passing events at home, or abroad; he wanted to know the news and the religious intelligence which the daily and weekly press furnished. He listened with pleasure to the reading of many books of history, biography, and general literature, and especially to devotional religious books, but he would readily turn from all these to the Bible, and was not satisfied unless several chapters were read to him daily. His love for the Bible was remarkable. He fed with delight upon its truths. He found in its teachings that which brought a peace, a comfort, a blessedness to his soul which he found nowhere else. The Lord Jesus Christ was to him a present and personal helper and friend, enabling him to bear cheerfully and uncomplainingly his infirmities and pains. Family worship he greatly enjoyed. Prayer to him was a reality and was often upon his lips; and nothing gave him more delight than to have a Christian friend come and pray with him, and converse upon religious themes. His sweet patience and submission to all God's dealings with him, revealed the depth and strength of his Christian character and attainments.

The Sabbath morning before his death, having had a night of suffering, he talked with his wife calmly and clearly about what she should do, expressing in fervent, loving words his appreciation of the tender care which she had given him; reminding her that it was time for family prayers, and when the Scriptures were read, the hymn, "My faith looks up to thee," was sung and prayer offered, he, with feeble and broken accents, joined in repeating the Lord's Prayer. After that there was read to him the chapters relating to the three men who were cast into that fiery furnace, and the Son of God walking with them—when he spoke of his being in the furnace and that Jesus would be with him, because he trusted in him.

He loved life, but met death without fear or anxiety, "knowing whom he had believed, and that he was able to keep that committed unto him against that day." "He walked with God and was not, for God took him."

G. S. F. SAVAGE.

LETTER FROM MISS DRYER.

MY DEAR MRS. HUBBARD: Though day by day we "walk through the valley of the shadow of death, and grow weary trying to fear no evil," we find it hard to let our friends pass on without us into the unclouded light and promised rest of heaven. In the home where we have loved them, we want to keep them ; and if we could, we certainly would deliver them from the power of the grave, and follow them on to gaze enraptured into the face of our Lord. But impenetrable mysteries divide us and them, and only faith finds consolation for us, in the fact that Jesus does not lose sight of those He loves. "Father, I will that they also, whom thou hast given me, be with me where I am," that comforts us ! "He'll not be in glory and leave us behind."

Dear Mr. Hubbard has gone to be "forever with the Lord."

The news surprised me. I thought he would stay with you longer. Your untiring, tender care of him, through these last, long months of dependence and child-like trust, filled his life with so much comfort that I, with others, have thought he might live months or even years longer ; and his marvelous endurance, his remarkable recuperation, his unflinching fortitude, and his patient resignation so stimulated our loving hopes that his departure finds us unprepared, even while he was ready and waiting.

Dear old man! so sweetly submissive to God, in his sore afflictions! Without a murmur he parted with those beautiful far-seeing eyes—eyes that had scanned the horizon of Lake Michigan and these wild prairies before Chicago thought of anchoring here—eyes for a long lifetime used to look right on and on for some new enterprise, some new good ; and when, after long suffering, he saw their light flicker and fade out, he never stopped looking, but right on to the celestial heights whence cometh everlasting help, he, with the sweetest simplicity of faith, still looked and endured, as seeing Him who is invisible.

I count it among my most precious privileges to have been so much in your family for more than a decade, and I shall always remember Mr. Hubbard's growing fondness for the word of God and for prayer, and his interest in our Christian work. So much loving kindness ; so many good words ; such hearty, pleasant welcomes ; for how much shall I cherish his memory and anticipate meeting him in heaven.

In Christian love and hope,

At Kilbourn, Wis., Sept. 23, 1886.   Emma Dryer.

(Extracts from Memorial of Sons of Vermont.)

GURDON SALTONSTALL HUBBARD.

Mr. Hubbard's life is remarkable for its covering the time in which Illinois has grown from an unimportant Territory into the fourth State of the Union in wealth and population ; in which Chicago has grown from a mere military station into the great city of the West ; and in these changes, Mr. Hubbard had an active and honorable part, passing away while held in high esteem by his fellow citizens for his adventurous and useful career. Of all the Sons of Vermont, none has done more for the State of his adoption than this man has done for Illinois.

* * * * * * *

In these sketches of his younger days, we may well introduce the personality of Mr. Hubbard. He was, when grown, of full height and of muscular build ; his nose was prominent, mouth large, lips firmly set, features irregular, expression serious, but not stern. He had great strength and tenacity.

* * * * * * *

Promptitude and courage were equally his characteristics. When Fort Dearborn was set on fire he swam the river to get to it, as no canoe was ready. On the outbreak of the Winnebago war of 1827, it was desired to send a messenger to the settlements south of Chicago and on the east side of the State. Mr. Hubbard was the volunteer messenger, and worked through great dangers and difficulties. Returning from Danville with fifty men, he came to the Vermilion River, which was swollen with rains, full, wide, and swift. The horses were driven into the stream to swim over, but only made a circuit and returned. Mr. Hubbard threw off his coat and mounted "Old Charley," a stout, steady, horse, which the rest might be induced to follow, and rode in, but in midstream Old Charley became unmanageable ; then Mr. Hubbard threw himself off on the upper side, caught the horse by the mane, and, swimming with his free hand, guided the animal across, while his friends were fearful he would be washed under the horse or be struck by its hoofs, and so lose his life.

* * * * * * * *

Mr. Hubbard finally settled in Chicago in 1833 or 1834. His business lay in many places at once, but now was centered here. From this time on, his career was not among dangers to life and limb, and his adventures were the peaceful ones of commerce. But as he had been the pioneer trader, he was still one of the foremost in all new things.

* * * * * * * ÷

While busy for the public in various ways he was making money for himself, and using it generously. The land speculations of 1836–37 he turned to good account. His losses in the great fire, when he was past the age of active effort to retrieve his fortunes, were great, but he still retained a handsome competence, at least. He lived in a plain, unostentatious way, from his natural tastes, and he was a familiar figure at the meetings of the Historical Society and of the Old Settlers. In politics he was a Whig, and afterwards a Republican.

* * * * * * * *

Lately Mr. Hubbard's health failed, both by age and by disease. Three years ago, an abscess compelled the removal of one eye; a year later the other was removed. Then the old pioneer, in the midst of the great city he had helped to build, weak as a child and helpless as an infant, sat two years in darkness, bearing his lot patiently, and waiting the stroke of death, which fell at last all gently on his hoary head.

———

(From the Chicago Times, September 18, 1886.)

GURDON S. HUBBARD'S FUNERAL.

IMPRESSIVE SERVICES, PARTICIPATED IN BY NEARLY ALL THE REMAINING PIONEERS OF CHICAGO.

The remains of Gurdon S. Hubbard, the pioneer, were consigned to their last resting place yesterday. The funeral, while quiet and unostentatious, was a notable one in many respects. In the morning the remains lay in the front parlor of the Hubbard residence, No. 143 Locust street.

The furneral services took place at the New England Congregational Church, Delaware place and Dearborn avenue. From the moment the doors were opened, a ceaseless stream of people entered, and at 2 o'clock every seat except those reserved for the mourners was occupied. The funeral party was met at the door by Rev. J. D. Wilson, pastor of St. John's Reformed Episcopal Church, of which Mr. Hubbard was a member. The pall-bearers were Ex-Governor William Bross, Judge John D. Caton, General Buckingham, Colonel John I. Bennett, G. M. Higginson, J. McGregor Adams, T. C. Dousman, and O. B. Green. The clergyman led the procession down the centre aisle, reciting in solemn tones the burial service of the Reformed Episcopal Church, beginning "I am the resurrection," etc., the congregation rising to their feet and the organ sending forth low, mournful notes, which added to the solemnity of the occasion.

The scene was one which must have made a strange and lasting impression upon those who were present. The congregation was an assemblage such as has seldom gathered in this or any other city. It was a sea of white heads, representing the men who came to Chicago when there was no Chicago, and who have lived to see the results of the work they began. Many of them were accompanied by their equally venerable wives. Other patriarchs sat alone, their helpmeets existing in memory only. With bowed heads they sat, their faces wearing an expression indicating that they were moved by deeper emotions than those occasioned by the loss of a friend and neighbor. Every mind must have felt an awakening of memories of early days, and of events which constitute the history of Chicago. On the platform behind the pulpit, sat Rev. Dr. R. W. Patterson, also an early settler, and the venerable Rev. Dr. Bascom, a Chicagoan since the thirties, who performed the marriage ceremony in 1843 which united the deceased and the widow who survives him.

When the reading of the service was concluded, the choir chanted the first twelve verses of the Ninetieth Psalm. Rev. Dr. Wilson read from the Scriptures, after which Rev. Dr. Patterson offered a fervent prayer. The choir followed by singing the hymn "Rock of Ages." Then Dr. Bascom briefly eulogized the deceased. He gave only an outline of his adventurous career, mentioning merely enough to quicken the memory of his hearers as to events most of them were familiar with. He laid stress upon the skill and fidelity of Mr. Hubbard, which eminently fitted him for the foundation of those business enterprises which have been the secret of the wonderful success of this city; his unfailing integrity, his trustworthiness and reliability. Dr. Bascom said that in all his years of residence in Chicago he had never heard one word impeaching Mr. Hubbard's honesty. He also eulogized him for his sense of justice and generosity, and his zeal as a churchman, having identified himself with the Reformed Episcopal Church at its formation, and remained a member until the time of his death. The speaker also gave an account of the last days and death of the deceased, remarking that those who mourned his death could look back with unspeakable satisfaction upon the fact that the manner of his death was peaceful. He was perfectly resigned, for months calmly awaiting the summons. During this period he was sustained by Christian hope, and enjoyed the rest and peace that he found at last, after an honorable and useful life. Mr. Bascom concluded by referring briefly to the lesson to be drawn from the demise of Mr. Hubbard, especially by most of those who heard him, whose advanced ages lent emphasis to it.

The closing prayer was offered by Rev. Arthur Little. After the benediction had been pronounced, the lid of the casket was removed, and the venerable men and women filed slowly by, to view for the last time the features of the deceased. There were very few who did not avail themselves of the privilege. The face of the departed wore a peaceful and almost life-like expression. Time had left few traces of its ravages. The face was that of a much younger and heartier man than many of those who gazed upon it. In a few minutes the lid of the casket was again finally closed, and the funeral procession retraced its steps. The interment was at Graceland, which was reached by carriages. There were no services at the cemetery other than the offering of a prayer by Rev. Arthur Little as the remains were consigned to the earth.